A White Christmas in Whistler

A winter in Whistler they'll never forget...

Family-run Cobalt Lake Resort is Whistler's most exclusive winter destination, but the past few Christmas seasons have seen little festive spirit following the tragic passing of the family matriarch.

But this year owner Brad Daniels and his daughter, Cassandra, are determined to recapture the holiday magic. And when two familiar faces from their pasts come calling, it's soon more than just the cold and snow that's making them shiver...

Read Brad and Faith's story in:
The Billionaire's Festive Reunion
By Cara Colter

Read Cassandra and Rayce's story in:
Their Midnight Mistletoe Kiss
By Michele Renae

Dear Reader,

This story is set at Whistler Blackcomb, a British Columbia resort that encompasses two mountains and is consistently ranked the number one ski destination in the world.

There is no Cobalt Lake Resort. This upscale boutique lodge was invented almost entirely by Michele Renae, my coconspirator on this duet.

Michele did such a brilliant job and got it so right that I found myself wishing it did exist, just so I could go to the s'more station by the lake and maybe catch a glimpse of a celebrity or two!

There is also no Feeney Pass and no secluded hot springs, though both these places are based on the kind of secrets small towns fiercely guard.

It was a pleasure to create this winter wonderland and this cast of characters with Michele. In book one, billionaire dad and widower Brad Daniels is given a second chance with his high school sweetheart. And in book two, his strong-willed, independent daughter, Cassandra, meets her match in a wounded champion ski hopeful, Rayce Ryan.

Michele and I invite you to join us for this partly truth and partly fiction—and wholly magical— White Christmas in Whistler.

Warmest wishes for the holidays!

Cara Colter

THE BILLIONAIRE'S
FESTIVE REUNION

CARA COLTER

ROMANCE

Harlequin®
ROMANCE

ISBN-13: 978-1-335-21613-7

The Billionaire's Festive Reunion

Recycling programs
for this product may
not exist in your area.

Harlequin Enterprises ULC
22 Adelaide St. West, 41st Floor
Toronto, Ontario M5H 4E3, Canada
www.Harlequin.com

Printed in U.S.A.

Cara Colter shares her home in beautiful British Columbia, Canada, with her husband of more than thirty years, an ancient crabby cat and several horses. She has three grown children and two grandsons.

Books by Cara Colter

Harlequin Romance

Blossom and Bliss Weddings

Second Chance Hawaiian Honeymoon
Hawaiian Nights with the Best Man

Matchmaker and the Manhattan Millionaire
His Cinderella Next Door
The Wedding Planner's Christmas Wish
Snowbound with the Prince
Bahamas Escape with the Best Man
Snowed In with the Billionaire
Winning Over the Brooding Billionaire
Accidentally Engaged to the Billionaire

Visit the Author Profile page
at Harlequin.com for more titles.

For the gifts of strength and hope

Kai 'Ehitu

Oh, yeah!

Praise for
Cara Colter

"Ms. Colter's writing style is one you will want to
continue to read. Her descriptions place you there....
This story does have a HEA but leaves
you wanting more."

—*Harlequin Junkie* on *His Convenient Royal Bride*

CHAPTER ONE

"CASSIE," BRAD DANIELS said to his daughter, "it's the third day of November. You just got the Halloween things put away. It's a little early to be working on details for Christmas, isn't it?"

His daughter—he was the only one allowed to call Cassandra "Cassie"—gave him the raised-eyebrow look. It was so like her mother, Cynthia—in charge, would not suffer fools lightly, a need for perfection—that he felt a shiver go up and down his spine.

He used to call the pair of them his dream team.

"Dad! We're actually *behind* where we should be. The tree for the front lobby needs to be a blue spruce and it has to be twenty-eight feet tall."

"One foot for each year of your life?" he asked dryly. "By the time you're my age we'll have to raise the ceiling."

He was treated to *the* look again.

"The height of the tree has nothing to do with my age, as you well know."

He grinned at her, just to assure her that, yes, he did well know.

She sighed. "Do you think you just go to the Boy Scout Christmas tree lot and get one of those the day before you need it?"

His daughter was beautiful, as her mother had been. Willowy, fine-featured, blue-eyed. She had done something with her hair that turned the natural blonde to an unearthly shade of platinum that was extraordinarily striking, even as he wondered, *What is this generation's rush to gray? It would come soon enough.*

As gorgeous as she was, Brad found her intensity—a kind of earnestness—to be the most compelling thing about Cassie. He felt a rush of tenderness for her.

The last two years there had been only the most desultory efforts at making Christmas the spectacular event that was expected of the Cobalt Lake Resort, the ski and accommodation destination in Whistler their family owned.

Christmas had been one of the things they were best known for before the loss of Cynthia in a horrible accident had left Brad and Cassie reeling.

This year, from the almost feverish look of determination sparking in those blue eyes, it was clear that Cassie was planning to make up for it, with the best Christmas ever.

"You're right," he conceded. "Bring on Christmas. I'm sorry. I won't be much help. I don't have any idea where the Christmas stuff is."

"Oh, Dad, it's all in the main storage room, on

shelves Mom labeled!" She looked at him indulgently. "Go back to running your empire, and I'll look after the resort. But remember, Christmas isn't a season, it's a feeling."

It was her favorite Christmas quote.

Brad groaned. "I have a *feeling* I'm going to be hearing that a lot over the next two months."

"It's not even two months."

"You're making my head hurt."

Cassie smiled at him then, and regarded him thoughtfully.

"Hey! Are you thinking I look old?"

"Not at all. You're only fifty-six. I was actually thinking how great gray hair looks on you."

His hair, salt-and-pepper when Cynthia died, had turned completely gray over the ensuing two years.

"Not every guy can say that," Cassie said affectionately, "but you look very distinguished, like Gregor Watson."

Watson, an actor, had just departed. He was one of many celebrities who had become a regular at Cobalt Lake, enjoying the upscale boutique nature of it, and that the resort was small enough they could go to great lengths to protect the privacy of their guests.

Security had had their work cut out for them this time, though. A couple of very determined members of the paparazzi had camped just outside the private property line, somehow having gotten wind of Watson's stay.

Security had nicknamed the most persistent of them "Gopher" because he kept popping out of various hiding places looking for the money shot.

He had not succeeded, however, in getting his prize—a photo of Watson, who had been named World's Sexiest Man about a million times.

"World's Sexiest Senior, here I come," Brad said dryly.

Cassie laughed.

As always, it was like the light had come on in his world. From the day Cassie had been born, it had been a source of amazement to him that two people as different as he and Cynthia could somehow create such a miracle.

It had been an accidental pregnancy. He remembered, clearly, on their twelfth anniversary, Cassie standing in front of them, hands on hips, doing the math.

"But I'm twelve! Did you get married because of *me*?"

"Oh, darling," Cynthia had said so smoothly. "We found out I was pregnant the very same day we had our engagement party. Which made it just about the best day of my whole life."

It was the tiniest of white lies, but what was important was that Cassie had been completely satisfied with the answer, and as far as Brad knew, it had never been mentioned again.

Brad sometimes wondered if that accidental pregnancy was part of what had sent his wife's need to be in control into overdrive. And now, he found himself wondering something else.

He felt he and Cynthia had enjoyed a good relationship, based on mutual respect for each other and love for their daughter.

Cynthia had loved Cobalt Lake, and as his parents aged, she had basically taken over the daily operations of the resort. By the time his parents had passed, she had been shifting the place to fit her vision.

Brad had always pursued other business interests, thinking of Cobalt Lake, even though it was a substantial holding, as more of a family hobby than a viable business venture.

Cynthia had proven him wrong on that front. She had taken the property from what had essentially been—despite the delusions of grandeur of his mother, Deirdre Daniels—a quaint little mom-and-pop ski hill to one of the most sought-after vacation destinations in Canada.

And Cassie seemed intent on taking it to the next level.

Had Cynthia been as happy with the marriage as he had been?

He had thought so. And then, two weeks ago, in search of a paperclip, he had looked through the desk his wife had always used. He had come across an envelope. It looked as if maybe it had been taped underneath the lip of the drawer, and the tape had dried over time, so that letter had whispered out of its hiding place, maybe even from him opening the drawer that had been closed for so long.

"You know, Dad," Cassie said carefully, drawing him back to the present, "maybe you're ready to meet some—"

"No," he said firmly, "I'm not."

The last thing he needed was his type A daughter thinking he needed to get back in the game. Much as he loved Cassie, Brad couldn't imagine anything worse than becoming one of her projects and having her devote her considerable energy to finding him a new partner.

He hoped his tone would be enough to make her back off, but, of course, that was not Cassie.

"Why not?" she pressed.

"I don't have the energy for it. If you think Christmas gives me a headache, you can't even imagine how I would feel sitting across a restaurant table with a perfect stranger, trying to think of things to say."

"It doesn't have to be like that. Traditional dating can be kind of lame. People need to think outside the box. Think how much you'd find out about someone if your first date was in a panic room!"

"I don't even know what that is." But he wasn't sure it could sound more awful than that.

"It's like a puzzle, only in real time. You get

locked in this room, and you have clues and you find your way—"

He pressed his temples. "Here comes the headache."

She laughed. "Okay, okay, backing off. But if you did decide you were ready, you could tell me, and I could help you."

By locking him in a room with a stranger?

Really? At least the name was apt. Panic.

"I'm just letting you know," she said softly, "that I wouldn't be mad, or resentful that you weren't going to mourn Mom forever. I'd be behind you one hundred per cent if you decided it was time to move on. It has been two years."

He knew that Cassie's grief for her mother was still raw, and so, while misplaced, it was such a generous offer.

Under all that drive, there it was—a loveliness of spirit that she tried to hide from the world, as if it was a weakness.

"Thanks, sweetie. You'll be the first to know if I need a captain for Team Brad."

Not that it will ever happen.

"Go find your Christmas decorations," he told her gently.

She waved a hand at him, and left in her typical flurry of energy.

After she was gone, Brad got up from his desk and reached for the jacket, which was hanging on the back of his office door. Time for a run. He'd always been a runner, and since Cynthia died, it brought him comfort he no longer got from the ski slopes. He called it his physical therapy.

It was cold and crisp today, the ice starting to form on the lake. He warmed up with a few stretches, but even when he started to run, his mind didn't clear.

He hated it that he had never questioned the strength of his and Cynthia's relationship while she'd been alive, or even after she died.

But that envelope, yellow with age, addressed in her firm hand...

Beloved

She had called him *dear* sometimes, and *darling* on occasion, but *beloved*? Never. So who was that letter for?

He had not opened it, or even decided if he would, but the questions it had stirred up were upsetting.

Was there someone she had loved before him? Had she married him only because of the pregnancy, because she thought she had to?

And an even worse thought: had the pregnancy been an accident at all? Or had his being a rising star in business—achieving billionaire status before he was thirty—been something that Cynthia, from a working-class background, wanted?

His mother had alluded to that possibility once or twice, until Brad had made it clear it would not be acceptable to him for his mother to air her habitual harsh judgments on the newest member of their family.

Cynthia had shown her mettle in very short order. She had left those humble beginnings behind her without a backward glance, sliding effortlessly into the world of prosperity that his business interests, more than the resort, at least at first, had provided.

She had been a perfect fit for that world, classy and refined. Okay, occasionally she'd overdone it, like using French words to sound chic. And when things reached her standard of perfection, she was fond of pronouncing them *marvelous.*

Still, any kind of accident, never mind pregnancy, was so out of her nature.

And yet, an accident had also killed her.

If she was happy, why had she loved those midnight skis by herself so much? Why had she taken a chance that night and gone into the avalanche zone?

Had she addressed a letter to *Beloved* before or after their marriage? Why had she kept it?

Should he open it, or respect the fact she had kept it secret? What if it blew apart everything he had believed about their marriage?

Brad shook off his thoughts, irritated with himself.

He had Cassie. And none of the rest of it mattered. At least not now.

It was colder out than he had thought it would be. His breath came out in icy puffs. He took the wide sidewalk that led him to the boardwalk that surrounded Cobalt Lake. He drank in the amazing view of Mount Sproatt. As always, the crisp air was a balm to his soul.

He caught sight of Gopher, hiding out in a group of trees just off the property line. He nodded to him, not letting on how annoying he found him, and thought to himself, *At least if he's here, unaware Gregor departed this morning, he's leaving someone else alone.*

He began to ramp up his speed, sprinting by one of the hot-chocolate-and-s'more stations provided by Cobalt Lake Resort. It was empty right now, but tonight the pathway would be lit up and people would be sipping hot drinks and taking— just as Cassie had planned—selfies against a magical backdrop that just happened to include the resort's logo.

It wasn't quite ski season, so there wouldn't be throngs yet. Christmas was the busiest time of year.

Brad noted the lake had formed quite a thick crust of ice around the edges. The water at the center was still open, though, and was the exact shade of dark blue that had earned the lake its name. If it stayed this cold, the lake would completely freeze over, and they'd be skating soon.

The ski portion of Cobalt Lake Resort was sandwiched between the two giants, Whistler Mountain and Blackcomb Peak, both of which he could see from here. Like their more well-known neighbors, Cobalt Lake was scheduled to open at the end of the month, snow conditions permitting.

They had a new ski pro, Rayce Ryan, arriving. He had been an Olympic gold contender before a skiing accident had shattered his leg.

Cynthia had always looked after hiring resort staff in the past, so this was Brad's first venture into it at Cobalt Lake. He hoped the new hire wouldn't come with the bitterness of dreams as shattered as his leg.

Skiing accidents had a way of changing how people felt. Brad lifted his eyes to the majesty of the mountains around him. All his life he had loved the mountains and the slopes so much. Cassie had been raised on skis.

Now, his daughter wouldn't ski at all.

And neither would he.

After Cynthia's death the resort had implemented a GPS tagging system for all their guests who ventured onto the slopes. It had already helped them find several skiers who had gone out of bounds and gotten lost.

But still, in the shadow of these mountains, Brad was aware how puny his defenses really were.

No matter what anyone thought, he was aware that the idea you could protect others was largely an illusion.

Again, he needed to shake off the shadows that threatened the beauty of the day. The sky was clear and blue, an osprey screeching and spreading its wings over the lake, the peaks of the mountains—Blackcomb, Whistler, Sproatt—shimmering with snow that had fallen at the higher altitude, but not down here.

Then, as if confirming Brad's thoughts about man's illusions about control, the perfection of the day was completely fractured. Suddenly, screams pierced the pristine mountain air.

CHAPTER TWO

THE SCREAMS HELD the pure and unmistakable—almost animalistic—sound of panic, the kind of terror of someone facing a threat to their very life.

It seemed to be coming from the area near the covered dock, which was located about halfway around the lake. Brad had already been running fast, but now he put on the jets, thankful that he was in great shape.

When he got to the dock, he pieced together what had happened in an instant. Out beyond the dock, on the ice toward that blue-black open water, a dog had broken through.

It looked as if a child—a girl, if the bright pink toque was any indication—was out there in the icy water with the dog.

The girl was screaming and scrabbling hard to get back on the ice, but every time she grabbed for it, the shelf broke away from her, like shattering glass. It didn't help her efforts that she wouldn't let go of the dog's collar.

A woman—the mother?—was racing back and

forth on shore, dog leash in hand, screaming hysterically.

"Call 911," Brad called to her firmly She stopped, her mouth frozen open, and stared at him blankly, tears streaming down a face distorted by pure terror.

"Call 911," he ordered her. "Do it now."

He was thankful for the hours and hours of relentless training as a volunteer with the search-and-rescue team.

When he was satisfied the woman was following his order, he looked around for something he could use as a reaching assist on the icy lake.

Search-and-rescue trained for this situation precisely, and so Brad found himself extraordinarily calm as he raced toward the flagpole at the end of the dock, pulled it from its holder and dropped down off the wooden platform onto the frozen surface of the lake, two feet below it.

He threw off his jacket. At first, where the ice was thick enough to support him, he ran flat out. But at the initial, barely discernable hint of the ice sagging under his weight, Brad dropped onto his belly. He tiger-crawled, using his elbows. He placed the pole well in front of him, horizontally, trying to distribute its weight across the ice as much as he could.

He inched closer and closer to the open water, to the flailing child and the frantic dog. The child was losing energy fast. The splashing was not so frenzied as it had been even moments ago, and the screaming had given way to a desperate gasping.

And still, she would not let go of the dog!

The ice creaked and groaned menacingly under Brad's weight.

And then, there was a giant crack.

It was sound like a gun going off and Brad braced himself to be plunged into the frigid water. He held his breath, but the ice, shockingly, held.

He inched forward again. Finally, he was nearly at the crumbling edge. Despite the fact that both the girl and the dog were tiny, Brad felt the surprise of how wrong he had been. This was no child in the water.

She was a mature woman, maybe his age, though the pink toque, with its huge pom-pom now completely bedraggled, looked like something a child might wear. Her soaked dark hair curled out from underneath it, and was plastered onto a face as white as the snow on the peaks that surrounded them. Her lips were already blue.

Her brown eyes, against all that white, looked huge, and filled with terror. The lashes were outlined in ice.

"You're going to be okay," he said firmly, deliberately keeping his voice calm and even. "Grab the pole."

He would not allow desperation to show in his voice, and he would not allow himself to get closer to the edge of the ice, even though he wanted to.

There was no sense in all three of them ending up in the water. In fact, that was the possibility that Brad had to guard against most.

So, not daring to go any closer to that fragile edge where ice met water, he shifted the position of the pole, skidded it across the ice and felt an exquisite sense of relief that it was long enough. She could reach it.

Crazy to notice, right now, that she was cute, rather than beautiful. There was something elfin in her features, even as contorted as they were by fear and shock.

"Let go of the dog," he ordered her.

Even freezing, even in this perilous situation, he could see a certain raw determination residing side by side with her terror.

"I'll get you first," he promised, "then I'll get the dog."

Only with that promise did she loosen her hold on the dog's collar and make saving herself a priority.

She grabbed the pole with soaked woolen mittens. He could see her strength was nearly gone. That realization made his own power, adrenaline-fueled, ramp up a notch.

Inch by careful inch, Brad pulled her, but the ice just kept breaking as the weight of her body hit it. Still, he stuck to his plan. He kept backing up, kept keeping himself from the point where the ice would give way. He held his position and the ice didn't break underneath him, though it groaned threateningly.

Finally, they reached a place where the ice was strong enough for him to yank her onto the surface and out of the cold black water.

She lay there, exhausted, like a beached seal. He heard a little sob of relief escape her.

The dog had stayed close to her, and was paddling furiously in water and chunks of broken ice.

"Stay on your belly. Spread out your weight and crawl to me."

Finally, she was right in front of him, her face down, crying, her breath coming in great heaves.

"The dog," she gasped through chattering teeth.

He had a decision to make. Rescuing the dog did not feel as if it should be a priority. She was already very close to hypothermic, though her chattering teeth told him she wasn't quite there, astonishingly.

Brad decided to make one attempt. If that did not work, he had to make saving the human life his primary goal.

"Do not move," he ordered her, and made his painstaking way back to the edge of the crumbling ice.

Knowing he had given himself one chance at this, he focused intensely. He managed to get the pole, lengthwise, underneath the dog. It took every bit of his strength to use the pole as a fulcrum point to lift the dog out of the water. The ice held under the pressure. The dog, thankfully, was one of those ridiculously tiny things, maybe a Pomeranian.

Brad brought his full weight down on his end of the pole. It acted like a teeter-totter and flipped the dog into the air and onto the ice.

The canine looked like a drowned rat when it dropped in front of him. It deftly evaded his effort to grab it, and gave him a few half-hearted challenging barks, the ungrateful beast. It shook itself indignantly. And then, all four paws going in separate directions, the dog took off running, slipping and sliding toward the shore.

Brad crawled back to the woman. She had not moved, her coat rising and falling with her huge intakes of breath.

"Thank you," she said, her voice a hoarse whisper.

He was pretty sure she meant for the rescue of the dog, not her.

They weren't off the ice yet, but he didn't let her know they were still in danger.

"We're good," he said, deliberately using the same soothing tone he might have once used on Cassie for a scraped knee. "Just listen very carefully to what I tell you."

She nodded.

"We're going to go together. We're not going to stand up. Not yet."

"I don't think I can move," she whispered.

"That's okay. I can. That's what I'm here for."

And suddenly it felt as if that was about the truest thing he had ever said. That he'd been put in this place, at this time, to do this.

He slid his arm under her soaked jacket. It was candy-floss-pink, like the toque. He got a good grip on her. He was immediately aware that he was pumping heat, from exertion and adrenaline, but that she was dangerously cold.

He pushed, pulled and cajoled her, both of them crawling back across the ice, one painful inch at a time. It probably took minutes, but it felt like hours.

Finally, the surface beneath them felt thick enough to take a chance. He got to his feet and crouched. He got his arms under her knees and around her shoulders and scooped her up.

Her wetness soaked into his pants and shirt—it was about the coldest thing he had ever felt, like picking up a block of ice.

Despite the fact that she was soaked, and maybe because his adrenaline was running so high, she felt as light as a feather.

She was limp, and yet with her cradled body against him, it felt as if the bottom was falling out of his world.

Because he saw pure strength there.

There was the vaguest tickle along his spine, of knowing her.

Deeply.

Maybe that's just how adrenaline made a person feel after sharing this kind of dramatic life event with a stranger.

As if you knew every single thing about a person.

Their heart.

Their soul.

"Thank you," she said again, but this time her voice was stronger.

It was when he heard her voice, for this second time, not whispering, not a croak of desperation, that he knew.

"Faith," he said, not quite knowing if he was speaking her name, or if that's what she—and this incident—was restoring him to, in a world where he had walked without that particular quality for a long, long time.

CHAPTER THREE

"FAITH CAMERON?"

It had been so long since anyone had called her that, that Faith felt faintly puzzled. Or maybe it was shock.

Who was she, again?

"Saint-John," she said, correcting her rescuer.

Her voice felt like it was far, far away, detached from her, coming from outside of herself. She was so cold. She had never been this cold in her entire life. She wondered, foggily, if maybe it went deeper than being cold.

Maybe she was dead.

There had been a moment out there in that icy water when she had resigned herself to fate. *This is it.* She had fully expected to die out there, the price to be paid for that foolish decision to go after the dog.

Not that it had felt like a decision.

She'd felt compelled, and had been out on the ice in an instant. It was as if her brain had turned off, and instinct had kicked in.

Though she would have thought instinct might

weigh a little more heavily on the self-preservation side. Faith mused that she could have spared a thought to her poor family. Hadn't they suffered enough?

She mulled over the possibility that she might be dead. She had read stories—scoffed at the time—of people who had died and been unaware of it.

Maybe all the rest of it—that man coming on his belly across the ice—had been a fabrication of hope.

And Faith, of all people, should know the dangers that lay in hoping.

So, possibly, she was dead. Somehow, it seemed totally unfair, that on death she would be greeted not by the husband she had spent thirty years with, Felix Saint-John, but by her first love.

But just as with hope, Faith Saint-John, should know life was unfair.

She squinted at her rescuer. Real? Or was her shocked mind fabricating? Or was he a greeter on the other side?

The other side had very sexy greeters if that was the case. Brad Daniels had changed, of course. Who didn't, thirty-plus years later?

His hair was completely gray, but the varying shades were exquisite, like storm clouds with the sun behind them. That same shade was in the faint stubble that speckled his flawlessly masculine cheeks and ever so slightly cleft chin. He had lines on his forehead, and crinkles around his eyes, but if anything, maturity had taken the raw handsomeness of his youth and refined it.

The lines around his eyes made him look as if he had laughed a lot. Once. Though laughter was the furthest thing from the intensity of his features at the moment.

His strength seemed unchanged, though. She remembered that about Brad Daniels. Strong, athletic, comfortable in his own body in a way so few people of that age were.

But those eyes! The same dark brown eyes that held a soul-deep calm that called to the very thing she thought she might have lost forever.

Some essential part of herself, gone.

Of course, she hadn't told her daughter that part. Only that she was returning to Whistler to fulfill the final wish of her father, Max—Maggie's grandfather—and have his ashes spread in his favorite place.

"Maybe you should wait until I can go with you," Maggie had said, but her daughter was a busy lawyer with two young children, which meant the right timing for her was a long way away. And Felix's illness had already delayed the granting of Max's request by far too long.

"Or maybe Sean could take some time off work."

Maggie was forever volunteering her good-natured firefighter husband for the Mom-needs-help projects, so much so that Faith referred to Sean as her saint-in-law rather than her son-in-law.

"How about Michael?" Maggie had suggested her brother.

For all her good intentions, there had been something mildly insulting about her daughter's insinuation that Faith wasn't up to making the journey on her own, so much so that Michael could be called home from his studies in Scotland.

Michael. Would he come home, if she asked? Of course. But would he come out of duty, or love?

Their poor family, so damaged.

No, asking Michael was complicated and out of the question.

"I'm going by myself," she had told her daughter firmly, shutting the door on further discussion even though she knew Maggie was only sensing what Faith was feeling. She was lost. Her name seemed to mock her, because that's what she had the least of after six years of giving everything she had to Felix. After six years of watching the man who had given her her whole life, and whom she had given her whole life to, morph into a stranger before her eyes.

And not a very nice stranger, at that.

"Unbelievable," Brad Daniels said gruffly, sternly, drawing Faith back, "that you would risk your life for your dog."

Faith frowned. If she was dead, that would mean Brad, greeting her at heaven's door, was dead, too. It seemed that the odds of her being welcomed to heaven by a lecture about dogs from an old boyfriend were ridiculously slim. On the other hand, what were the odds of being rescued from the cold jaws of death by her first love?

She managed to smile weakly. She couldn't take her eyes off his face. She wanted to touch it, to determine if he was real, but she couldn't move. Her hands were so cold that she doubted she would be able to feel his skin—what she thought would be the delightful texture of those rough whiskers—anyway.

"You know what's even more unbelievable?" she asked, finally managing to answer him. "It's not my dog."

Was he taking her clothes off? It seemed he was, dispensing with her sopping jacket, and then, quickly, the sodden blouse underneath.

She couldn't be dead! Would she care that he left her bra in place, left her some semblance of modesty, if she was dead?

In a flash, his own jacket was around her. That scent could be described as heavenly, so maybe... Then his hands were rubbing the outside of that jacket, firmly, relentlessly.

It was a good thing she couldn't feel anything, because she was pretty sure if she could, her every resolve would be weakening under his firm touch. At least his physical touch made her very aware that yes, she was definitely alive!

"The ambulance is coming," Brad said, cocking his head. "Almost here."

And sure enough, Faith could hear sirens getting louder and louder.

There was a woman hovering around Brad's shoulder, clutching the wet dog and sobbing. "Thank you. Thank you. I don't know how to thank you."

And then Brad was not at her side. Peripherally, Faith was aware of him putting his body squarely between her and someone else. A man, with a very bulky camera. Brad seemed highly annoyed. He blocked the man from taking a picture, and she could hear the sharpness of his tone, if not the actual words he was saying.

The ambulance was here. So much commotion! People asking her questions, more sirens in the distance, the dog giving sharp, bossy little barks. Then, she was being lifted onto a stretcher.

And Brad was beside her again, holding her hand, and the world felt quite, quite still.

"Why?" he asked her, with a kind of urgency, as if he might never see her again. "Why did you risk your life to save a stranger's dog?"

"Its name was Felix," she said, and then she was suddenly aware of the fresh pain she could have brought her family with that impulsive decision. She was crying, aware the tears felt unbearably hot on her cold face.

He let go of her hand and the first responders took his place.

"I'll come with you," Brad said as they moved the stretcher toward the waiting ambulance.

"No," she said firmly. So firmly it stopped him in his tracks. She tried for a softer tone. "It's okay. Really."

The stretcher was being loaded, the doors were shutting and the only warm part of her was where the tears had tracked down her cheeks. And the part she least wanted to be warm was the part around her heart, which she had resolved must be kept frozen.

So that it could never be hurt again.

That's why she had said no to Brad coming with her in the ambulance. She didn't want to see him again for the exact reason that she wanted to see him again.

Her heart was being pulled in two different directions: come back to life, and stay numb.

The next hour—or maybe more—went by in a blur as hospital staff worked on warming her up. Finally, they left her, wrapped in a cocoon of a heated blanket.

Beyond exhausted, she slept.

Faith woke up feeling the most beautiful sensation of warmth, but also a feeling of disorientation. That smell...

She opened her eyes, slowly. She saw a light blue privacy curtain and an IV pole, and heard the unmistakable sounds of a hospital—codes being called, shoes on squeaky floors, the hum of machinery. The smell was that mixture of disinfectant and despair that she had come to know too well.

She struggled to sit up. If there was one place she did not want to be…

There was a strong hand across her arm, staying her. She turned her head. Brad Daniels was sitting in a chair beside the hospital bed.

"Hey," he said.

It was really unfair that he had aged so well. He was one of those men who was getting better as he got older. It felt like such a terrible weakness that she was glad he was here, despite the fact she had asked him not to come.

"Hey," she said back, and sank against a cushion he put behind her back. The effort it had taken to sit up drained her, so she closed her eyes again, and just let an exquisite feeling of contentment float through her, replacing that moment of panic when she'd realized where she was.

"Feeling okay?" he asked.

"Yes, so good. Warm. You didn't have to come."

"Of course, I didn't *have* to. But I knew your clothes were wet."

She suddenly remembered him pulling her soaked clothes off her. It felt horribly embarrassing. She kept her eyes closed.

"I wasn't sure where you were staying so I didn't know where to go to retrieve some dry things for you to put on when they discharge you."

He laid a package on her lap, and she opened her eyes again, and looked at it, instead of him. Looking at him made her feel weak.

Swamped by memories.

Of a younger Brad, his lips on hers, awakening something in her that she had never known before.

Or since, if she was going to be completely honest about it.

She told herself, firmly, that what she'd had with Felix was so much better than fickle, youthful passion. It was steadiness, security.

"I've got your jacket and sweater, but I didn't bring them here. I think it's going to take about a year for that jacket to dry."

The package was wrapped in brown paper and tied with hemp twine, the way very exclusive shops would have done it. The paper had *Cobalt Lake Resort Boutique* subtly embossed on it, and a little green sticker that attested to its environmental friendliness.

She had barely cried since Felix had died, six months ago. Today, she was making up for it. Now, as she slid her finger under the twine, it felt as if she was, once again, choking back tears.

Faith drew out the items, one by one. Brad had obviously gone way beyond her basic needs. There was a beautiful new down jacket and a soft woolen toque in the same shade of sage green.

This was followed by a pair of navy blue yoga slacks, a plain T-shirt and a light zip-up hoodie that matched the slacks. Like the packaging, each item had a sticker on it attesting to how it was doing its part to save the world.

"Sorry about the leisure wear," he said. "They're kind of one-size-fits-all, so it felt like a good bet, since I don't know your sizes."

"No," she said, "it's perfect."

For someone who didn't know her sizes, the last items in the bag were underwear—a lacy white bra and matching panties. A quick glance at the label showed them to be sustainably produced, breathtakingly expensive and her size *exactly*.

She dared a glance at Brad and saw he was blushing, ever so slightly. It was endearing. Was he remembering things best left in the past?

She quickly tucked those items under the brown paper and ran her fingers over that raised, tasteful embossing.

"So is the Cobalt Lake Resort still in your family, Brad?"

"Of course," he said, reminding her he was one of those enviable people who had always known what his future held.

"I don't remember there being a boutique."

"It was one of my wife's ideas."

It was one of the very questions she had wanted answered about him. Of course, he was married. No surprise there. The Daniels family was nothing if not traditional. In fact, it was *good* that he was married, a comfortable barrier for the niggling of attraction she felt for him, still, after all these years.

Or maybe it wasn't attraction at all. She was probably experiencing some kind of psychological phenomenon, some kind of bonding to the man who had, after all, just saved her life.

Faith slid a look at his ring finger to confirm. A band of gold rested there.

"Did your wife help you pick things for me?" That would put the *sexy* things in a different light.

He twisted the band.

"She died," he said. "Two years ago."

So much for the different light. He had chosen those things.

Still, Faith noticed Brad's tone was flat, as if he was deliberately trying to strip the emotion from it. But she saw an anguish, the kind that she was very familiar with, flash through the deep brown of his eyes.

Something in her went very still. What were the chances of this? Of the craziness of their reunion and then this interesting twist? That both of them had lost their life partners?

"I'm so sorry," she said quietly.

So many questions. How had his wife died? Did they have children? What directions had his career taken him in? Were his parents still alive?

Had he been happy with his choices? Or had his family's expectations—his domineering mother, to be precise—dictated them to him?

Suddenly, she felt as if she wanted to know everything about him. What had the last three decades held for him?

She could see the same curiosity in him as those dark eyes rested on her, inquisitive.

Her close call in the lake had made her feel weak. His thoughtfulness had made her feel weaker yet.

Faith was appalled to find she craved connection with Brad Daniels.

But life had taught her the inevitable link between connection and loss—even the companionship of a cat was destined to cause pain—and she could not leave her poor battered heart vulnerable to that.

She had vowed that her children, and her grandchildren, would be enough for her at this stage of her life, even as her daughter, Maggie, looked somewhat panicked at the idea of being her mother's raison d'être.

Mom. You've got to find yourself again.

Maggie wanted her to find herself, but ironically, didn't even want her to travel alone to the place she had spent some of her high-school years.

And maybe that concern was not completely unjustified. Look at the chance she had taken, racing out on that ice for a dog.

Faith felt a sudden jolt of panic. Maggie!

CHAPTER FOUR

"WHAT TIME IS IT?" Faith asked, after twisting her neck to look frantically for a clock in the hospital cubicle.

Brad slid back his cuff to reveal a gorgeous watch. While she and her husband—he'd been a university professor, until his retirement, and she had been a teacher—had always been comfortable, there had never been room for watches like that in their lives.

Brad's watch was probably worth more than the down payment on their beloved downtown Toronto bay-and-gable, pre-World-War-Two-constructed house had been!

"It's just after five."

"Oh! I was supposed to let my daughter know when I got here."

When Faith had arrived in Whistler her hotel room had not been ready so she had decided to delay calling Maggie until she could do so from the comfort of her room. Since she had not been able to check in, she had left her suitcase—with her dad's ashes inside it—in a secure storage room.

"Mom," Maggie had said, "I don't think you can just travel with, er, human remains. Or spread them wherever you want. I think you have to get permits."

Her daughter, the lawyer, would think of such things. But for once in her life, Faith was not going to do it right, or follow the rules. Her father would have approved. One of Max's favorite expressions had been "it's easier to beg forgiveness than ask permission."

So Faith had left the suitcase and then gone for that fateful walk around Cobalt Lake.

Another thought struck her, and her rising sense of panic increased.

"Where's my phone?" she asked. "My purse?"

Brad's brow furrowed, as he obviously was trying to remember the scene.

"I didn't have my purse when you pulled me out of the water?"

"Definitely not then."

"I hope I left it on the shore."

"I don't recall seeing a purse there. But I wasn't looking for one."

"What if my purse—and my phone—are at the bottom of Cobalt Lake?"

"You likely threw the purse down," he said, and there was something about him that was just so reassuring. "Do you remember where you entered the lake? Off the dock? Your purse might be there."

"I don't know where I went out onto the ice. Or if I threw or dropped the purse as I ran. It's all kind of a blur. All I remember, clearly, is that woman screaming for Felix."

"The dog."

"Yes."

"And something more?" he asked softly.

After a moment, she nodded.

"Who is Felix?" Brad asked, in a voice that felt as if it could call all her secrets from her.

She sighed.

"That was my husband's name. He died."

Brad drew in a sharp breath as he, too, recognized the coincidence in their shared tragedies.

Faith was aware she didn't need to offer anything else. But the close call, the weariness, now the loss of her purse—one blow after another—seemed to be lowering her barriers.

"Recently?" he asked quietly.

"Six months ago."

"I'm so sorry, Faith."

"Felix, my husband, had a horrible condition. A form of dementia most people had never heard of, until that action film star got it. It was a behavioral variant. It affected his personality, his judgment, his empathy."

She was slightly in awe of herself for managing to sound so clinical about something that had been so utterly devastating.

"Oh, Faith." Brad did not appear to be falling

for her matter-of-fact tone. His deep voice was gravelly and showed genuine caring. His eyes on hers seemed to invite her to fall into what they offered: the understanding of someone who had also loved and lost.

She ordered herself not to say one more word. She ordered herself to remember the danger of connections, particularly to another human being.

Particularly given her shared history with Brad. But even as she tried to warn herself of the dangers, she kept talking. She glanced at the IV dripping into her arm. Was it possible there was something in that?

"He left me a long time before he actually died. I couldn't save him. No matter what I did, he just drifted further and further away from me."

The clinical dispassion was leaving her voice. There was a little wobble in it. This would be a really good time to stop talking.

"I couldn't save him," she whispered, "but when I heard that woman calling his name, it felt like maybe I could save something."

Why was she saying this? It had to be the IV making her say things she shouldn't. Feel things she shouldn't. For instance, she shouldn't feel as if she *knew* Brad. As if she could trust him with her grief and vulnerability, as she had trusted no one else, not even her daughter, or her son. You didn't know someone because they had been your *first*.

Well over thirty years ago.

There was probably nothing resembling truth in those first passionate encounters between Faith and Brad.

But even if she had not known him fully back then, she could not deny she the raw genuineness in him, coming out on that ice and rescuing her. Everything he was had been on full display, with no filters. Strong, brave, compassionate, wise, willing to put himself at risk for someone he had thought was a stranger.

It had also felt like raw truth in his eyes when he had told her about the death of his wife.

Still, obviously, she was in some kind of shock, or on drugs, which had made her blurt out personal details of her life like that.

And then, her defenses completely crumpled, and she was crying *again.*

Faith had an awful thought. What if she had come all this way, thinking fulfilling her father's final wish would help her find herself, and the hard truth was that the self she would find was weak and needy and given to sharing confidences with people she didn't know?

Well, that was not exactly true.

She *knew* Brad Daniels.

Or a version of him.

She didn't know him now. Ridiculous to feel as if she did, based on his heroics on the ice.

"Scoot over," he said, and she could no more

disobey this command than the ones he had given her out there on Cobalt Lake.

He came up on the narrow bed beside her. Despite all her warnings to herself about the dangers of connecting, she did not tell him no, she did not push him away, she did not try to avoid contact with him.

She *liked* the feeling of his weight sinking down on the bed beside her. She *liked* his scent—subtle, masculine, mountainy—tickling around her nose.

He didn't draw back the thin blanket that covered her, and so his thigh was on one side of it, and hers on the other.

Still, the contact—the connection—was there. Subtle heat from his leg, her leg lying against the hard length of solid muscle.

And she liked that, too.

It had been so long since she had shared a moment like this with another human being. Except her grandchildren—Maggie's two daughters, Chloe and Tanya, four and six—who snuggled into her as she read them bedtime stories.

She had been away from home less than a full day, and suddenly she felt melancholy, homesick.

"I think there's something in the IV drip," she said with a loud sniff.

"There probably is," he agreed.

"I'm glad we got that sorted. That I'm being drugged. That I'm not like this. At all."

"Like what?" he asked huskily.

"You know. Needy. Weak. Talkative."

"I don't see you as any of those things," he assured her softly, then he drew her head to the exquisite broadness of his shoulder and let her cry as he murmured soothing words. It felt as if she had never known anyone in quite the same way she knew Brad Daniels.

"I'm really not—"

"Shh, give yourself a break. You've had a shock. You're probably mainlining muscle-relaxants."

She giggled at the suggestion, and relaxed into the comfort he was offering.

Finally, and with what seemed like just a touch of reluctance, Brad extricated himself from the bed and handed her some tissues.

She was glad it had been quite some time since she had put on makeup, because had it survived the lake it would not have survived this deluge of tears.

While she dabbed at her eyes and tried to stop the heaving of her chest, she watched as Brad took charge of everything. He was a man that had so obviously come fully into himself. He'd always been confident, but now maturity had added weight to that confidence. She could not help but admire how he handled himself as he made calls to the resort and sent staff out to look for her purse and her phone.

His manner was friendly, but also firm. There was an unmistakable power in him. There was an invisible line, even on the phone, that made him one-hundred-per cent the boss.

This is what she needed to remember, since it felt so good to just surrender to being the one taken care of—once she had been staff at his family resort.

And his mother had not had the people skills her son had. Deirdre Daniels—always Mrs. Daniels to the staff—had been rigid and condescending, possibly the worst boss Faith had ever had.

And that was before Mrs. Daniels had made it known, in no uncertain terms, that there was no room for a chalet girl—and probably particularly one with the last name Cameron—to have a place in her son's future.

But all that seemed a long time ago and far away as Faith let this next-generation Daniels take charge of her life.

When he was done making his calls, Brad handed her his phone. "Call your daughter," he said. "Let her know you're okay."

He kindly exited the room to give her some privacy.

His phone was still warm where it had been cupped in his hand. What an utterly ridiculous thing to find appealing.

She glared accusingly at the IV drip before punching in Maggie's number. Of course, her daughter did not pick up, either because of the time difference—bath time for the babies, there was that sensation of homesickness again—or because it was coming up as an unknown number. Either way was a blessing, because Faith did not want to confess to her daughter that she had nearly brought more tragedy on the family, or tell her about the predicament she currently found herself in, or the circumstances that had led up to it.

It would just confirm all those doubts that had flashed through Maggie's eyes when Faith had announced her mission. She could practically hear the exasperated, worried, *Oh, Mom.*

"Hi, honey, safe in Whistler," Faith said with artificial cheer, leaving a voice-mail message. She glanced around the cubicle, glad it wasn't the video chat she would normally have used to connect with Maggie, Chloe and Tanya. The backdrop would have been a dead giveaway, that left to her own devices for the first time in years, Faith had managed to make a mess of it.

"Sorry to be letting you know so late. I seem to have misplaced my phone."

I knew she shouldn't go by herself, Maggie would say to Sean, when she heard that message. *How do you misplace your phone?*

"I bumped into a high-school friend who loaned me theirs," Faith continued. "I'll check in with you tomorrow."

She disconnected, thankful that her son, Michael, was away at university in Scotland and there was no need to keep him updated as to what

was going on. She'd sent him a text about her up-
coming travels, but she was not sure it had even
registered with him.

Faith had the feeling that Michael had been
grateful for the physical distance separating them
when Felix was ill. The last time he had come
home it had been a fiasco. It felt as if his sense of
family had been deeply compromised by the trials
of the last few years, and he had chosen a chilly
withdrawal. When she'd told him she was thinking about selling the house he'd grown up in, he
hadn't responded at all, as if that part of life—and
happier times—was far behind him.

And then there was Maggie, who cared too
much.

How could she begin to repair so much dam-
age to her family? Could she?

She sighed, and looked at Brad's phone, willing to take advantage of the diversion from the
troubled state of her own thoughts. She was *not*
the kind of person who would give in to the temptation to check out a few photos on the unlocked
device.

Of course, she wasn't the kind of person who
dashed out on the ice after a dog, either. Or unloaded emotional baggage in front of strangers.

Maybe she didn't know who she was at all anymore. Wasn't that at least part of the purpose of
this mission that already seemed to be going so
badly awry?

Of course, nobody would be more delighted by things going *awry* than her free-spirited dad.

Faith decided, even if she was choosing a new her, it wouldn't be someone who snooped on someone else's phone. She did like the wallpaper on Brad's lock screen, though. It showed a beautiful young woman with silvery hair, sitting in a mountain meadow and looking toward the camera with undisguised affection.

His daughter, she assumed, studying the similarities in the bone structure. The woman didn't exactly look happy—she had lost her mother, after all—but there was both strength and confidence in the set of her chin, and shoulders, in the directness of her gaze.

He had raised his children well.

She scoffed at herself for reaching that conclusion on the basis of one photo. She didn't even know if he had a daughter, or how many children there were.

It could even be a niece, though that wouldn't explain the resemblance. Brad had been an only child, like Faith, so if it was a niece, it was on his wife's side.

When the door of her hospital room squeaked open, she hastily put the phone on the table tray in front of her as if she was a spy who had been caught looking at a file!

CHAPTER FIVE

IT WAS A doctor and a nurse, not Brad, who came into Faith's room. It was a sign of how much the world had changed since she was young—in good ways—that the doctor was a woman and the nurse was a man.

The nurse, who introduced himself as Adam, began to remove the IV.

"Is there something in that?" Faith asked him, as the doctor laid a very cold stethoscope on her chest.

"Yes, it's a heated intravenous solution of salt water. It helped warm your blood."

"And that's all?" Faith heard faint skepticism in her tone.

"That's it," Adam said with a smile. "If you're feeling not quite yourself—"

Whatever that was, she thought silently.

"—it's probably because your body sustained quite the shock. You're very lucky."

Lucky. Of course, she was. She had made a stupid, irresponsible decision and been saved from the consequences.

And yet, she was deeply suspicious of luck. Luck—chance, fate—had also selected her and Felix for a journey into heartbreak so breathtakingly painful nothing could have ever prepared her for it.

Still, with her rescue from the icy water of Cobalt Lake, her poor family had been saved from yet another blow, and for that she really did need to be grateful.

Even as she hoped they would never find out what she had done. The very thought of Maggie's tone, the look that would be on her face, made her cringe inwardly.

"Thank you for all your hard work," Faith said to the medical team. "I feel lovely now."

Except for the fact she had just discovered she had no excuse for confiding so deeply in Brad, for accepting the comfort of his body next to hers on the bed, his broad shoulder to rest her head on.

Faith was stunned by how much she missed those kinds of everyday intimacies. But those yearnings could make a person weak when they most needed to be strong.

"You'll need to take it easy for the next few days, but I think you're good to go," the doctor said.

But that was a dilemma. Go where? With no purse, no ID, no credit card, no phone? She wouldn't even have clothes if Brad had not supplied them.

The medical team left the room and Faith got

out of bed, shocked by her lack of strength. Her legs felt as boneless as pudding.

She ducked into the tiny bathroom that adjoined the room with the clothes that Brad had given her. She pulled off the hospital gown—even that small effort sucked the strength from her—and sorted through the items.

She found herself blushing at his choice of undergarments. So feminine. Maybe even sexy. She had given up on sexy a long time ago, even before Felix got ill. Comfort had seemed way more important.

But even if it had been a long time since she'd worn anything but the most utilitarian underwear, she was too old to blush.

Still, she'd spent thirty years with the same man, so putting on undergarments purchased by her old high-school sweetheart felt oddly intimate, just like Brad beside her in that bed. But how had he gotten the sizes so right?

Her sense of embarrassment deepened as she recalled him yanking those sopping, cold clothes off her on the shore of the lake.

She hoped he was so busy in rescuer mode that he hadn't noticed that she wasn't eighteen anymore. Was rounder than the lithe teenager she had been.

But Brad wasn't the kind of guy who missed a thing.

Which included the scars of life, stretch marks and wrinkles, and things she had really thought she would never be brave enough to show another man in her life.

And yet, in this really lovely underwear, it seemed as if all her flaws were minimized. For the first time in a very long time, Faith felt exquisitely feminine. She realized why a woman might be tempted to spend so much money on lingerie.

She slipped on the yoga slacks and top. Both were products of a well-known designer—made from sustainable bamboo—and, as Brad had promised, one size fitted all, though maybe it was a bit on the snug side, hugging the curves of a body that had not been in a yoga class for at least twenty years.

Would yoga classes be part of her journey to find herself? Faith glanced in the terrible warped mirror above the sink.

The harsh hospital light wasn't helping, but she really did look awful. Her natural curls—dark brown threaded through with the odd strand of gray—were crushed to her head in some places and sticking straight up in others.

She pulled on the toque—the label said it was hand-knit by a local artisan—and that hid the worst of it. Her lips still looked faintly blue and she looked as pale as the death she had come close to experiencing.

She was annoyed at herself that she felt like she would have killed to get her hands on that little makeup kit tucked away in her suitcase.

Faith exited the bathroom. The small effort to get dressed had increased the sensation of heaviness in her limbs. She sank onto the edge of the bed, and ran her hand over the bamboo fabric of the slacks, trying to think what to do.

First and foremost, she had to break this sense of connection with Brad.

They were now, and always had been, from different worlds.

He was from a world of wealth and good taste. His mother had made it abundantly clear that a chalet girl—Mrs. Daniels's euphemism for a chambermaid—had better not have designs on her son.

Those had been her words, spat out, snooty and cuttingly judgmental. Her tone had been lady-of-the-manor to maid-who-emptied-the-pots.

Have designs.

Those words could not have come at a worst moment in Faith's life. Despite the bliss of loving Brad, real-life problems had been pressing up against her. Only a few days before, her dad had confessed he'd gambled away the money he had scrimped and saved for her college fund for as long as she could remember.

She had never seen Max cry before, but he had cried when he had told her, "I thought it was a sure thing. I thought I could at least double that money. That you could have gone off to UVic and lived like a princess instead of a pauper. It was a pony named Faithful Fate. I thought it was a sign…"

Could Mrs. Daniels have known about Max Cameron's terrible mistake? It seemed she did. Whistler remained very much a small town.

Because Mrs. Daniels had then held out the single carrot that Faith had been unable to resist. She had offered to pay all Faith's expenses—tuition, housing and a small allowance—for her entire four years at a prestigious university in Eastern Canada, a long, long way from where Brad would be going to school at the University of Victoria, on Vancouver Island.

Faith had been accepted at UVic, as well, but even with scholarships, after her dad's confession, she had been contemplating the financial aspects of pursuing a higher education with terror. She would be on her own. Though she had always excelled in academics—she loved to learn and knew early on that she wanted to be a teacher— she knew no matter how she stretched, or how many part-time jobs she managed to land, she wasn't going to be able to do it.

And, of course, by accepting Mrs. Daniels's offer, she hoped to somehow alleviate her father's shame and pain over his awful mistake, too.

To fix it.

Look, Dad, it all worked out.

Faith had insecurities—and plenty of them— before those words, and that offer, from Mrs. Daniels. By the time they'd arrived in Whistler, when she was in grade eleven, they had moved so many times.

Despite his horrible mistake gambling away her college money, Max had had only one addiction. It had been spectacular. It wasn't as if he didn't like booze and gambling, but those paled in comparison to his grand obsession.

Max Cameron had been a powder hound. It always seemed the place he thought he would be happiest was wherever he wasn't.

And so they had followed the promise of snow. Max had worked at Lake Louise, Sunshine Village, Aspen, Deer Valley, Jackson Hole and a multitude of others, loving how the one guaranteed perk of working at a ski resort was either free or discounted skiing.

He'd had great dreams for Faith, but she had never developed his love of the sport, possibly because it had cost her so much in terms of stability.

Instead, she had loved books and school. Max had eventually given up on a ski-racing career for her, referring to her affectionately as his little bookworm.

Books, though, didn't provide a complete barrier from the knowledge she had grown up with, of how resort towns worked. She was well aware that she and her father were on the bottom rung of a caste system, and that was before his many eccentric escapades were figured in.

Ski villages hosted very rich people who came for extended stays or owned the fanciest homes, and availed themselves to the posh resort lifestyles. They skied and hiked and went to spas, and sipped expensive wine in front of fires. If they had families, their children mostly went to private schools.

Then there were the business owners, like the Danielses in Whistler, who sold accommodations, or fine art, or exquisite furnishings, or designer clothes made out of bamboo. They were heavily community-minded, and that included supporting the local schools.

At the bottom of the resort-town heap were the people, Max said, with a grin and a shrug of his shoulders. Like the Camerons, who actually kept everything running, the maids and the store clerks and the lifties and the mountain guides and the ski instructors.

These people couldn't actually afford to live in most of the famous ski resorts in North America, unless they were lucky enough to get staff housing. Otherwise, it was trailer parks and basements suites, or houses shared with other employees. Faith had grown up experiencing all of those options at various times.

Max had been a seasonal worker, a chair-lift mechanic, and the absolute best at what he did. He had also been a true free spirit who had never conformed to what society expected from him.

He had been a single dad since Faith's mother had died when she was three. He had embraced that role with a startling joie de vivre.

She could remember him bursting in the door of her first-grade Christmas concert—where had that been, Big Sky in Montana?—looking panicked because he was late, his hands still black with grease and dressed in his work coveralls.

But the pride on his face, the love in that lopsided grin, had made her world. Though as she got older, it hadn't always felt like enough. Her dad's work could be as sporadic and unpredictable as he himself was. Especially in high school, when she had become aware money was tight and taken the job at Cobalt Lake to help out.

She'd been the new girl—again—and didn't have the right clothes or shoes, couldn't afford a good haircut and certainly didn't live at the right address. The money she'd earned helped pay the rent, it didn't buy baubles.

And so, when Brad Daniels—wealthy, athletic, popular, a member of the Whistler elite—had first shown interest in her, Faith Cameron, daughter of a lift mechanic and a lowly employee at his family's resort, she truly had felt like Cinderella, with a real live prince and a chance to dance at the ball.

She'd met him at school, not the resort. Having many experiences with moving, Faith had known the way to meet people was to join something, preferably not something that cost extra money.

And so she had joined the school paper…and been mortified when her first assignment was to interview the athlete of the month, who had been Brad.

With his good looks and his athletic prowess, she had been expecting arrogance and superiority. Instead, she had found someone who seemed unaware of his social standing, or of hers. He was funny, humble and genuinely interested in people. He was one of the easiest people she had ever talked to. Sometimes it felt as if he was interviewing her, since he was so interested in all the different places she had lived.

Originally intimidated by him, she'd asked him for half an hour of his time. An hour later they had ended up going for sodas together at a local café.

He'd asked her, almost shyly, at the end of that time, if he could see her again.

She'd taken a deep breath, and admitted she worked as a chalet girl at his family resort. She would never forget the slow, sweet smile that had come across his face.

"Oh, that's wonderful," he'd said. "It means I'll see even more of you."

As if her station in life, and his, meant absolutely nothing to him. And it never seemed as if it had.

Faith had allowed herself to get caught up in the fairy tale of first love and to believe good things could happen to a girl like her.

But then, as it turned out, even if Brad genuinely did not care about the differences in their circumstances, *somebody* had, and she cared very much.

Brad's mother.

She had flung those stinging, life-altering words at Faith. And then made her that offer.

That offer. She knew it was a deal with the devil.

Three days had passed without eating or sleeping. Crying until her eyes swelled nearly shut.

And then, Faith had done what she had to do. She accepted the terms—all of them—dictated by Mrs. Daniels.

Dealing with moving was nothing new to her. But dealing with heartbreak was. She missed Brad so much. She was dying to call him, to explain, to just hear his voice.

And Faith missed her dad, as well. He had been the constant in her life, and yet he seemed broken by the choice he had made, and the choices she had made as a result. Nothing she said or did when she called him seemed to make him feel better. Brad was out of her life and her father was drifting away from her.

She threw herself into her studies, blocking out heartache, trying to outrun that not-good-enough feeling. That, and the guilty awareness that she had somehow sold out. She had done what her father would never have approved of. Chosen security over happiness, the safe way over the un-mapped route.

It had taken years to feel she belonged in her solidly middle-class life, especially with Max in the background, leaving Whistler at the same time she had, and going back to Banff. And then to Colorado. For a while, he'd been in Europe.

She'd had to send him airfare to come to her wedding, the first time he had met Felix. He'd taken her aside and suggested she "rethink" Felix, proclaiming him as dull as yesterday's porridge. Though he'd never been much of a drinker, he'd made an exception on that occasion. Max had gotten drunk and made a toast to a "boring and conventional life."

She'd been glad to put Max back on the plane, glad his presence in her boring, conventional life was sporadic. Because she loved *everything* about that life.

She had the life she had always hoped for— her own career as an elementary-school teacher, a husband who was stable and doting and, finally, motherhood.

Faith *loved* every single thing about family life and motherhood.

She loved it that she and Felix had aspired to the most ordinary of dreams. To have children, to buy their own house, to have a warm holiday in the middle of winter and to save their money so that Maggie and Michael could go to university, worry-free.

That life—those, oh, so ordinary goals—had

slowly made Faith *finally* feel she was okay, that she was worthy of good things.

But then those good things had been snatched from her, in a dizzying flurry of tragedies. Her father had been diagnosed with liver disease—after ignoring the symptoms for years—and come home to her, only to die within weeks.

At about the same time, Felix's baffling changes in behavior had accelerated alarmingly.

And so, all those old insecurities seemed as if they had not been put to rest at all. They had just waited, patiently, for this past boyfriend to show up in her life and make her feel, at fifty-five, when she had really hoped to be beyond such things, insecure all over again.

It was not exactly, she thought wryly, what she had come back to Whistler for—to find herself in the grip of events that had happened well over three decades ago!

And she needed to remember the goal in her quest for discovery. Despite the insecurities of growing up in class-divided resort enclaves, when she was young, she had been so aware of her strength.

There had been a period when she had felt as if she could overcome any obstacle. During those romantic months of first love with Brad, at the end of their senior year, Faith had had a sense of being on fire with life, immersed in the moment, embracing the possibility that anything could happen.

So the ghosts of her former self had drawn her back here. That insecure girl wanted to find the roots of her self-doubts, exacerbated by Felix's illness; and that confident girl who thought she could do anything wanted to be coaxed back out.

Brad chose that moment to come back into the room. In light of the thoughts she had just had, Faith saw him through a new filter.

He carried himself with an enviable vigor for life. The air around him was practically shimmering with his amazing energy. He had an unshakable sense of himself, an innate self-confidence. It was in everything about him, in the way he dressed, in the way he carried himself, even in the polished cut of his silver hair.

The color of his hair was undeniably sexy on him. He looked like Gregor Watson. Only better, because he carried his looks without a hint of arrogance.

She did not want to be noticing anything *sexy* about Brad Daniels. But, given their recent close encounters—and his choice of underwear for her—how could she not?

"They tell me they're releasing you. Can I give you a lift?"

Of course, he could not give her a lift! She had to stop this right now! But what was she going to do? Walk back to her hotel? When her legs felt as if they were barely functioning? And then what?

"Yes, a lift would be nice. I'm not sure what I'll do about checking in. Without my wallet."

He tilted his head at her.

"I just arrived here in Whistler a few hours ago. The room wasn't quite ready for me so I left my luggage, but I'll have to see what the hotel has to say now that I'm without ID or a credit card."

He considered this.

"Maybe you should come back to Cobalt Lake with me until your things are found."

Such a bad idea.

Terrible.

Given the softness he was making her feel in places that had gone hard. That she had hoped were impenetrable for forever more.

That's exactly what she was afraid of.

That and the growing connection, if she allowed him to rescue her again.

"I keep a cottage at Cobalt exclusively for use of visiting executives. There's no one in it currently. You'd be welcome to it, until we sort out your difficulties."

It was a relief that he wasn't actually asking her to stay with him. That relief was somewhat nullified by his casual use of the word *we*.

It had been such a long time since she'd had a partner to help her with her decisions and difficulties. The kids had done their best, but it wasn't the same as this.

Someone to lean on.

"No," she said, with convincing firmness, "I've put you out quite enough. If you drop me at my hotel, I'll figure it out from there. I'm sure they've had guests lose things before."

CHAPTER SIX

BRAD WAS TRYING very hard not to stare at Faith. The outfit he'd hastily picked up for her from the boutique was made for someone with straighter lines than hers.

Her generous curves seemed beautifully womanly to him. Cynthia had been an athlete, all hard muscle and sinewy strength. She had never had a hair out of place, and her makeup had always been perfect, even when she stepped in, fresh off the slopes.

Faith, understandably, was having a bad-hair moment, that even the toque couldn't hide. Wayward curls were escaping out from under it, some sticking up, some flattened against her temples. Her face was makeup-free and her skin was so pale. It made her eyes look huge.

There was something distinctly waiflike about her. She was definitely vulnerable and he could not forgive himself if he just dropped her off at her hotel to cope when she was in a more fragile state than she seemed to realize.

There was something else about her, that he remembered from their shared past. In high school, that place that celebrated *sameness*, particularly in girls—same hair, same clothes, same fingernail polish—Faith had stood out.

She had not been the same.

The first time he'd ever even noticed her was when she'd interviewed him for the school paper.

Her wayward curls, that tentative smile, those huge earnest eyes, the *questions*. Nothing he'd been expecting.

If you could have a conversation with anyone, living or dead, who would you choose?

If you were stranded on a deserted island, who would you want to be stranded with?

At that point, he'd known Faith Cameron five minutes, and the answer to both questions had been *you*. Not that he had dared to admit that out loud. He had never been so completely captivated before.

And maybe, he realized, not since, either. Was there anything in the world that matched the thrill of first love?

There had been something about her...and still was. Something fresh and wholesome, wonderfully original and surprising. His mind settled on the word *real*.

He remembered, with startling clarity, the first time he had tasted her lips, how sweet and plump they had been, how she had been both innocent and eager. As he himself had been. They had discovered the brand-new world of passion together, with curiosity and boldness and reverence.

And joy.

Maybe especially joy.

He was appalled with himself when he realized he was comparing Faith to Cynthia. His guilt was instantaneous. Still, he needed to reassure Faith in no uncertain terms.

"It's not putting me out, Faith."

Brad contemplated the storm of feelings—oh, those most dangerous of things—that he was feeling. *Put out* was not one of them.

Aside from the guilt of catching himself comparing his wife to another woman, Faith's rescue had breathed to life a dying spark within him. The spark was that need a man had to be the warrior—to protect those around him.

Rationally, he knew he had nothing to do with Cynthia's decisions, the ones that had led to her accident and death, but a part of him felt, acutely, a sense of failure.

A powerlessness no man wanted to feel.

He had carried that sense of failure and powerlessness within him until that very moment he had succeeded in pulling Faith from the water.

Is that why he didn't want to let her go now? He wanted to relish this sense of having wrestled with fate, and won, this time?

He was being too complicated, he admonished himself sternly.

Faith Cameron—no, Saint-John now—had made it abundantly clear she didn't want any more help from him. Or at least, that's what her *words* said. But the *feeling*—there was that pesky thing again—that he was getting from her couldn't be more different than those words she had just spoken.

He wasn't sure what had possessed him to climb into that bed with her, and to take her in his arms, to comfort her, but he had, and it had changed everything.

Coupled with the rescue, he felt protective of her, something he had not felt for a long time, and something he needed to remind himself he had failed at—spectacularly—once before.

Still, it was pretty simple.

She was an old friend. She'd had a shock. She didn't have a wallet or a purse or a phone.

On top of all that, Gopher had been on the front steps of the hospital when Brad arrived.

"I got some great photos of you and that woman out on the lake," the paparazzo had said. "And the dog. The dog angle is the kind of thing that could make it go viral. It could be my break. Maybe even better than some shots of Gregor."

Without saying a word, Brad had pivoted and turned back to the parking lot.

"You could be a hero! I've got a really good

writer interested in the story. She's here in Whistler, too, at the moment. But time is of the essence. Nobody will care about it a week from now."

Yay, Brad thought, still walking away.

"If I could just talk to you for a minute, it could make you famous."

Brad could not think of one thing he would like less than being famous. He always felt such pity for Gregor Watson, who could no longer do one normal thing without being hounded. But Gopher, a man who made his living preying on that whole cult of fame, would probably never understand that.

"And her. What's her name?" the annoying man had asked.

Brad had reached his vehicle with Gopher, undeterred, on his heels. He'd snarled at him, "Get lost, before I call the police."

He'd gotten back in his vehicle and made it look as if he was driving away, but in actual fact, he'd pulled into the lane at the side of the hospital.

A staff member on break had recognized him, and used his pass to open the locked side entrance.

"Good job out there on the lake, Mr. Daniels."

Oh, boy, it had never been one of his ambitions to be a hero in a small town.

Still, the notoriety cemented his desire to protect Faith. If ever a person needed a rescue, it was her, and if ever a person had needed to be a rescuer, it was him.

"Um…" he said to Faith now, after she had turned down his offer of accommodation "Do you want the good news or the bad news?"

They had often teased each other with that very phrase in those months they had been together as a couple in high school. He saw recognition dawn in her face, and a smile touched her lips.

It wasn't until she smiled that he realized how haunted she was, not just by the events of the day, but by what life had handed her with her husband's illness.

It wasn't until she smiled that he realized how much he wanted to make her smile again.

"The good news," she decided.

"Damn it," he said.

"What?"

"There isn't actually any good news."

And then she laughed, and it was exactly as he remembered her laughter being, a pure light in a world he hadn't even realized was dark.

"First of all, there's a reporter out on the front steps of the hospital who seems to think your rescue could be story of the year."

"A local reporter?" she asked.

"Unfortunately, no. He's been hanging around trying to catch Gregor Watson."

"The actor, Gregor Watson?"

"Yes, but he's not here anymore, a fact that hasn't caught up with Gopher."

"Gopher?"

"My security staff nicknamed the photographer. Gregor stays at Cobalt when he comes."

"Oh," she said, digesting that, looking at him as if there were facets to him that she had not considered.

"I don't want my children to *ever* find out what happened. Maggie, in particular, would put me on the doddering-old-fool watch list."

He smiled. "My daughter can also be pretty unforgiving of what she perceives as my senior-moment transgressions."

"I think I saw her picture on your lock screen when you loaned me your phone. She's extraordinary, Brad. Is she your only child?"

He felt that rush of pride that Cassandra always made him feel. "Yes, she is. She really is beautiful."

"Yes, I saw that. But there was something about the way she held herself that made me think she's very confident and strong, a credit to you."

He felt so pleased by those observations.

"She's a great young woman, even if she doesn't allow me to use the word *typing*."

Faith chuckled. "I'm not allowed to correct spelling and punctuation in texts."

"I bet you're encouraged *not* to use them, right?"

"So right! And I was a teacher. It's like swallowing nails not to add a comma here and there. To plunk down a sentence with no capitals. To not scream in frustration at autocorrect."

"You became a teacher," he said, pleased. "That was your dream."

"Yes, it was. grade three and four. When they're still so lovely, and nearly fall over dead if they see you in the grocery store because they can't imagine Mrs. Saint-John actually eats."

It was his turn to laugh, but then he made himself get down to business.

"Aside from Gopher, the other bad news is that I know they can't allow you to check in at the hotel without a photo identification, and a credit card." He said this carefully, speaking from his long experience in the hospitality industry.

She contemplated that for a moment, then drew in a deep breath. "I should probably just go home. I can do what I came here to do another time."

It occurred to him, almost shockingly, that he did not know where *home* was for her.

"Do you think you could check flights to Toronto for me?"

He made no move toward his phone.

"I should just get you to take me back to Vancouver. To the airport." She blushed. "Or arrange for someone to do it. Sorry. It's a long trip. You're obviously a busy guy. Not a chauffeur. It's not like you're staff."

Why had she said it like that, with that funny little inflection in her voice on the word *staff*?

"Actually, if I could just borrow a bit of money from you," she said quickly, "I'll take the sea-to-sky shuttle to the airport. That's how I got here. It's a beautiful drive."

But that drive was two hours long, and it was evident to him that Faith was beyond tired, and practically swaying on her feet. She was in no condition to be making these kinds of decisions.

He decided not to tell her the resort had a helicopter at their disposal—another reason the celebrities loved visiting them—that could get her to Vancouver International in under half an hour.

But getting her to the airport was one thing, getting her on a plane was another thing altogether.

"Um… I hate to be the one to break this to you—" *not really* "—but if you don't have the right documents to check in to a hotel, you don't have the right documents to get on an airplane, either."

Brad watched as Faith figured out exactly how bad a pickle she was in.

"Oh, no," she whispered.

She didn't have to look quite that aghast that she was realizing she was highly dependent on him, at the moment.

"On the other hand, even if you could get on a plane, if you went home early, there would be lots of questions from Maggie, I'm sure."

She gave him a grateful look, for thinking of that angle, or remembering her daughter's name, he wasn't quite sure.

"How long were you planning on staying?"

She had to think about it for a minute.

"I'll be leaving Friday…if I can get things sorted out."

"Then let me look after you," he suggested, gruffly. "Whistler's still a good place, despite how much it has grown. I have every confidence your purse will be found or turned in, but until it is, just come to Cobalt."

Her shoulders heaved. "I guess I have no choice," she said with such genuine reluctance it stung him.

She reminded him, a little bit, of that ungrateful dog, barking at him after its rescue.

He frowned suddenly, remembering their senior year, and how they had discovered each other. He remembered the richness and excitement of first love. *That* feeling—made breathless by someone else's presence—that no matter where you went in life, no matter what other thrills you experienced, that one could never be replicated.

Firsts.

And then he remembered she had hurt him.

And that had been a first, too. His first broken heart. Brad reached back over the years, and the details were surprisingly sharp.

He'd been astonished to find a curt note from her, left at the front desk of the hotel, saying she was leaving Whistler to pursue her life and she wished him well with his.

He'd called her home phone—no cell phones back then—but no one had answered.

He'd driven by that trailer she and her dad, Max, lived in about a thousand times, but it had appeared to have been totally abandoned.

When he'd finally found the nerve to go the door, Max had been shirtless and swigging a beer. His eyes were red-rimmed and he'd looked at Brad with a sadness, as if someone had died.

"She's gone, buddy. Off to school."

"UVic?"

For a moment, had something like pity crossed that man's sorrowful features?

"No, she changed her mind."

Brad didn't want to beg, but he had. A phone number, an address, *anything.*

But her father had shut the door in his face.

Brad looked at Faith now, and saw in her expression exactly what he had always seen in her. Despite her reluctance to accept his help, there was an unguarded softness in her eyes and around the plumpness of the bottom lip she was chewing. She wasn't like that snappy little dog at all. He could see what she was: a person of innate integrity and kindness.

And yet, that note from decades ago had not been either.

The opposite, in fact.

A reminder that he had not *really* known Faith,

any more than he suspected now, that he had ever really known his wife.

So, a warning.

To look after Faith, if she accepted his invitation, but to keep his distance, too. To protect himself from his inability to read the heart of the female species.

CHAPTER SEVEN

BRAD, WITH OLD-WORLD manners that did not surprise Faith, held open the door of his vehicle for her. They had exited the hospital through a side door, in case Gopher was still camped out at the front entrance.

She shuddered at the thought.

"What?" Brad asked her.

"Just thinking of my daughter finding out about my escapades because they've become front-page news," she told him.

"It's not 'front-page news' anymore," he informed her solemnly. "It's *going viral.*"

And then they were both laughing. It was the second time he had made her laugh. She thought she could probably count the number of times she had laughed in the last five years on one hand.

She noticed his vehicle was one of those very sophisticated, very large all-terrain sports vehicles. She had to step up to get into it.

She slid into the deep leather seat, and Brad shut her door with a click. He came around to the driver's side and started the vehicle with the push of a button. It hummed quietly to life and Faith was enveloped in a sense of luxury.

The scent was heavenly—part Brad, part new vehicle. The seats were heated, the interior was filled with the notes of a lovely acoustic guitar from a sound system so good the guitarist might have been in the back seat.

Like Brad's watch, the vehicle sharply highlighted the differences in their worlds. Faith drove a subcompact in Toronto. Felix had never been able to part with his old Volvo, which had been secondhand when he'd acquired it.

It was now nearly six o'clock, and the peaks surrounding the village had disappeared behind the shroud of absolute darkness that one only experienced in the mountains.

Brad pulled away from the hospital. "What hotel?"

She told him and then said, "The SUV is a bit of a surprise. If the boutique packaging is any indication, Cobalt Lake seems to have embraced all things eco-friendly."

He glanced over at her and grinned. "It seems like one of those gas-guzzling pigs, doesn't it?"

Had she sounded judgmental? She hadn't meant to. She'd just been trying to make conversation. "I'm sure it's necessary around the resort, and for unpredictable winter conditions."

"A bigger vehicle with four-wheel drive is necessary, but this is actually an experimental vehicle, a prototype that we'd like to produce if we can figure out how to get the costs down. It's an innovation based on hydrogen-fuel technologies."

"You own a vehicle company?" she said with surprise. "I thought you had inherited your family business, the Cobalt Lake Resort?"

"I did, but it never was at the forefront of my interests. I might have even let it go completely after my parents died."

"I'm sorry. I didn't know your parents were gone," Faith said, guiltily happy there would be no chance encounters with an aging Mrs. Daniels at the resort.

"My wife, Cynthia, loved it, and managed to drag Cobalt Lake Resort, kicking and screaming, into the twenty-first century. My daughter, Cassandra, does most of the day-to-day management of it now, so that I can focus on other things."

She heard the pride in his voice at the mention of his daughter's name. She had a sudden horrible memory of Felix brushing past Maggie, pretending she wasn't there, inexplicable hostility stamped in his features.

A reminder of how terribly wrong love could go.

She felt as if she had been punched and left breathless, as was so often the way when these memories surfaced. Thankfully, it was dark in the car, and Brad had that lovely gift for conversation.

"I'm a part owner of the hydrogen-fueled-vehicle company. I'm actually part owner in quite a few ventures. In university, I discovered I had a gift for sniffing out innovation, and figuring out which, of the millions of them, had potential."

This was said without even a hint of conceit, but with the enthusiasm of a man who truly loved his work.

"Right now, the most exciting project I'm involved in is developing an exoskeleton for human beings. It has amazing ramifications for the severely disabled."

Faith glanced over at him. In the light of the dashboard, she could see that he was, despite his losses, all of the things she was not. As in: fully engaged in life.

He pulled up in front of the hotel. "No, you stay there. I'll go get your things."

"I'm sure if they won't let me check in without ID, they're not going to hand over my luggage to a complete stranger."

He raised an amused eyebrow at her. "Stay here."

She watched him go, riveted by the presence he radiated. She saw him lift a hand to people he recognized, exchange quick greetings, once even stopping for a moment. There was a sense of him being where he belonged, and knowing it, in a way she found enviable.

Finally, Brad slipped through the doors of her hotel.

While he was gone, she put down her window and breathed in deeply. The mountain air had a texture to it—sweet, pure—that she had only ever experienced in these mountain villages.

Whistler Village had always been high-end, even in her growing-up years, but the atmosphere had morphed into something out of a fairy tale, an unlikely combination of cozy mountain meets cosmopolitan posh.

There was no snow and it wasn't anywhere near Christmas, and yet there was that holiday feeling with white lights threaded through the branches of every tree, and outlining every window, awning, railing and building.

The sounds of laughter, people chattering, cutlery rattling, glasses clinking, came in her open window and filled the crisp mountain air with happy sounds. Despite the chill of the evening, Whistler celebrated the outdoors in all seasons.

The patio areas of cafés, pubs and wine bars were open, the tables full, heat lamps glowing bright orange. People, colorfully dressed in parkas and toques and scarves, drifted in and out of shops, laden down with parcels. The was an air or excitement, prosperity and vitality.

A few minutes later, Brad emerged, carrying her suitcase by its handle. He was so strong it had not even occurred to him, apparently, to use the wheels to drag it along.

Again, she noticed him exchanging greetings.

He opened the back gate of the vehicle and tossed the suitcase in. He would live in that world of very expensive luggage. But if he had noticed hers was slightly travel-worn and certainly not a brand name, it didn't show in his face.

"I hope they at least put up a fight before they handed that over to you," she said.

"Yes, I did a tug-of-war with the desk clerk."

He laughed. His laughter was so wonderful. It shimmered with a promise of a life that held laughter again.

She wasn't sure if that was a good thing or a bad thing, but she found herself leaning toward a good thing.

"I'm pretty well-known around town," he said. "Not the one they're watching for to make off with luggage that doesn't belong to them. I seem to be especially well-known now. At least three people mentioned what happened at Cobalt Lake this afternoon. It's the talk of the town."

"Oh, no."

"Don't worry," he said, "I'll keep you out of the glare of the spotlight until this all blows over. In a week—or less, if we're lucky—they'll have moved on to something else. Last week the talk of the town was the stray-cat problem. The dog rescue is a little more riveting for now. But next week, who knows? 'Skunk family takes up residence under Banker's Bar? Bear misses memo on hibernation and is chasing tourists through Lost Lake Park..."'

He was making her laugh again. And then they were on the familiar rode to Brad's family resort.

If Faith thought Whistler had changed, nothing could have prepared her for Cobalt Lake.

Like Whistler, it was like something out of a fairy tale, every tree and every walkway lit up with millions of tiny white lights.

The lodge and grounds had been given a complete facelift.

No wonder Gregor Watson stayed here, and Brad appeared to be on a first-name basis with him!

"But where are the chalets?" she whispered, catching glimpses of gorgeous little cottages seeded among the stands of evergreen trees at the base of the ski hill.

"Oh, those old A-frames?"

Yes, the ones, she had cleaned to his mother's exacting standards.

"They hadn't been built properly, and were starting to have issues as they aged. Mold. Frozen pipes. Roof leaks. Decks that couldn't withstand the snow load. Cynthia replaced them with these cottages, one at a time, over the years. All the A-frames are gone now."

He skirted the main lodge, and took a side road

that curved through a forest grove, lit with fairy lights. It looked amazing. Faith could just imagine how magical everything would look when it snowed.

Brad stopped in front of a delightful structure, set well away from the other cottages. Faith went to open her door, but he lifted his hand, ever so subtly, and then came around and opened her door for her.

Again, such an old-world courtesy, and she *loved* it.

She stood looking at the cottage, trying not to let her mouth fall open. In what world was *this* a cottage?

It was a house, and a beautiful one at that. A tasteful sign showed it had been named Wolf's Song, and Faith remembered the name of the ski run directly behind it was Timber Wolf.

The Cobalt Lake Resort had always named their cabins, but they'd had cutesy names like All Decked Out, Misty Morning Magic, Mountain Standard Time and the Bear Cub Club. The new name signified a change in direction that was also more than evident in the new face of the resort.

A wide, curved stamped concrete walkway led the way, through manicured shrub beds that held plants chosen to keep color, even in the winter— emerald cedars, miniature mountain pine, dwarf burning bush.

The "cottage" had a craftsman-like style with an

imposing stone-and-wood facade. Open trusses, huge and wooden, held up the roof over the covered entryway. Two flickering gas lanterns framed the large front door, which looked majestic and antique.

Brad carried her one shabby suitcase onto the porch and she followed him up the wide staircase. The spacious deck area had four deeply cushioned outdoor chairs on it, black-and-white-plaid blankets draped artfully over them.

Something brushed by her feet, and Faith gave a little squeal and stumbled back toward the staircase.

Brad dropped her suitcase and had her in a second.

"That darn cat," he said, annoyed.

Out of the corner of her eye, she saw a white form dashing away.

He didn't let her go, right away. She felt his nearness, breathed in his scent, and his strength.

"You're destined to rescue me today," she said. She intended it to sound light, but it didn't feel light. She was marveling at the sensation of having someone to lean on, of not having to rely on her own—admittedly quite wobbly—strength.

"My pleasure," he said, stepping away from her. "That cat! Such a nuisance. It's been hanging around here since the summer."

She suspected the cat was being used as a distraction, as if he, too, had felt a shiver of something white-hot with promise pass between them.

Brad punched in a code, and opened the door. He set down the suitcase inside. That poor suitcase had never looked more forlorn, and like it didn't belong.

"It's probably not the kind of luggage you're accustomed to," Faith ventured, as a way to tame down the white-hot-with-promise thoughts.

Brad looked down at the suitcase, genuinely baffled. "What?"

"Like not Louis Vuitton. Or even Samsonite, for that matter."

"Oh," he said, cocking his head and looking at her suitcase, then dismissing it with a shrug. "They all look the same to me. Cynthia picked all that stuff."

It occurred to Faith that maybe she was exaggerating the differences between them—focusing on the watch, the car, the luggage—as a form of self-protection.

But then Brad flicked on a light switch, and stood back to let her pass him. Faith stood in the foyer. No, she definitely was not exaggerating the differences in their worlds. The interior of the cottage was like something on the front cover of a lifestyle magazine.

CHAPTER EIGHT

"THIS IS INCREDIBLE," Faith breathed.

The decor was mountain-lodge, but in the most upscale way imaginable. It was a completely open plan, with expansive hardwood floors, huge windows, a floor-to-ceiling stacked stone fireplace. Logs crackled invitingly inside the firebox.

"You like it," Brad said, pleased.

And it seemed that was all that mattered to him, that she liked it. There seemed to be no ego—*look what I have*—in his statement at all.

"What's not to like?" she asked. "Did your wife do this, too?"

"She had a designer."

Faith had grown up in rented trailers and basement suites, with secondhand furniture and left-behind art hanging crookedly on walls.

She remembered her and Felix tackling projects in what they had thought would be their first house, with a kind of reckless enthusiasm. It had been modest, large enough, but in much need of repair. Its main selling point had been the location—walking distance to the historic St. George campus of the University of Toronto, where Felix worked, and the elementary school where she worked.

But it had also appealed because it had been on a block lined with mature trees that gave them shade in the summer, and that gave them birds to feed all winter. How Felix had adored coming up with increasingly complex plans to try and keep the squirrels from those feeders!

They had lovingly fixed the leaky basement and painted walls, and prepared nurseries, and bought throw cushions. They went through awful decorating stages, like sponge-painting walls and a Southwest theme and Scandinavian-style furniture.

When the time had come when they could have moved on, Faith, possibly because of her gypsy childhood, had been completely unable to let it go.

Their starter home became their forever home.

It had never—not once—looked like this, or even close to this.

But somehow, they had created a sense of home. And had so much fun doing it. She remembered the time they had painted the nursery in preparation for Michael moving out of the bassinette beside their bed. The color on the paint chip had been fine, but on the walls it looked hideous.

"My," Felix had said, mildly, "he's going to feel as if he's growing up inside an aquarium."

"Lucky boy," she'd said, deadpan.

And then, with paint in their hair and on the tips of their noses, they had started to laugh, and they had laughed until they were rolling on the floor.

Faith suddenly felt sorry for Brad. She bet he'd never had a moment like that in his entire life, poor guy.

She slipped off her shoes.

"You don't have to take off your shoes," he said.

"I can't imagine anything more un-Canadian than leaving your shoes on," she told him. Not to even mention the thought of scratching those beautiful floors could give her nightmares.

She let the great room draw her into it. "Who lit the fire?"

"Oh, I called ahead. One of the staff got it ready."

There it was again. *The staff.* Just in case she had any ideas about trying to forget the divide between their two worlds.

Their house had a fireplace. It had never drafted properly and every time they tried to light it, the whole house filled up with smoke and the fire detectors went off.

And for some reason, that was a good memory, too.

She realized, startled, that *good* memories had not been part of how she remembered Felix, so far.

She and Felix could not have afforded to stay in

a place like this in a million years. What would it cost? A thousand dollars a night? Conservatively?

Even if they could have afforded it, she suspected they would have never done it, not even for a special treat. No, they would have opted to spend the money on a new furnace. Or bringing the kids home from university for Christmas, or building up their retirement savings accounts.

Yes, now that she thought about it, it was definitely building the retirement savings account that would have won out instead of a night in a fancy hotel. How important that had been to Felix… She shook off the feeling of sadness that was trying to edge in on her sense of genuine enjoyment of these posh surroundings, her surprise at finding herself here.

"Sit down," Brad invited Faith. "You look dead on your feet."

Not the impression one wanted to give, but she felt the same way she looked, and moved into the great room and sank into one of the deep inviting armchairs that faced the fireplace.

"I'll put this in the bedroom," he said and took her suitcase through a door off the main entrance. "I'm going to head over the lodge. I'll rustle up a cell phone for you, and bring something over to eat."

He was gone before she realized she had not said no.

In fact, she felt powerless to say no.

Faith settled more deeply into the comfort of the chair and enjoyed the flickering beauty of the fire, and the lovely light it cast over the stunning cottage interior.

She let her gaze roam around the room. Despite how undeniably grand it was, with its soaring ceilings, gorgeous light fixtures and priceless art, the room was somehow extremely cozy and welcoming. That's what designers did, she supposed.

She could see those professional touches in the upscale kitchen that was at the far end of the open space. It had a dizzying array of stainless-steel, high-end cabinets, stunning light fixtures. An entire bank of windows looked out toward the ski slopes, though the slopes were just a dark shadow at the moment.

Fresh flowers and a fruit basket were sitting in the center of an expanse of Italian marble that was the kitchen island.

Sadly, it felt like a kitchen not a single person had ever baked cookies in. She thought of Chloe and Tanya, standing on chairs beside her in her kitchen, as covered in cookie dough as she and Felix had once been covered in paint.

Still, as Faith looked back to the fire, she was aware of feeling slightly stunned to find herself ensconced in Wolf's Song.

Since Felix's diagnosis—no, way before that, because things had to become quite alarming before you even sought a diagnosis—she had felt as if she was being thrust deeper and deeper into a carnival funhouse.

Why were they even called that? Those places that kept your world feeling tilted and off balance. Those places of warped mirrors and hideous surprises and false exits. Those places where the panic rose in you as you became more and more lost in the mazes, and became more and more convinced you could never find a way out.

And yet here she was. She had popped out. Been released from the "fun" house nightmare.

She was sitting in this gorgeous cottage, in front of this soothing fire, only because her beloved husband, by now a stranger to her, had died.

How terrible, Faith thought, to feel relieved. To be so *glad* to be sitting here, instead of immersed in the day-to-day tragedies of living with someone who had been afflicted with bvFTD, or behavioral frontotemporal dementia.

She had been flattened by it. Numbed.

Was it the shock of hitting the frigid water that had jolted her out of the trance she had been in? She was aware that, starting this afternoon, for the first time, she had a real sense of leaving it behind her.

This is *exactly* what Maggie had wanted for her. Well, maybe without the dog, the icy lake and the near-death experience.

But this feeling of the flatness leaving her.

Being in Brad's cottage felt just like being warmed up in the hospital.

That's what the memory of Felix and his obsession with the retirement savings account had tried—unsuccessfully, it would seem—to edge out.

A sense of the life force creeping back into her. She felt alive.

And, okay, just a little bit frightened by the feelings Brad was drawing out of her. He had suffered a loss, too. Why did he still seem so vital? So engaged with life? It made her feel as if he had a secret that she needed to know.

She shouldn't really feel compelled to uncover any of Brad Daniels's secrets. In fact, it was dangerous. It felt as if, with the tiniest little shove, things between them might be right back where they had been when they were teenagers. Terrifying, indeed.

But why be afraid?

Hadn't life already done its very worst to her?

"Dad," Cassandra said over his phone, "what on earth is going on?"

Brad's phone was blowing up. It seemed every single person in Whistler wanted to know what had happened on Cobalt Lake this afternoon. He looked at it, alarmed, as the message counter kept ticking up. Fifty-six messages? Fifty-seven. Fifty-eight.

He'd put it on silent mode, but the phone was programmed to let Cassandra's calls come through. Even if he was screening everyone in the world—which it seemed he was at the moment—he always tried to be available to his daughter.

The signal was really bad—probably because Brad was in the wine cellar. The lodge had its own wine cellar, but this one, below their residence, had been Cynthia's private enclave.

He didn't even know when he'd last been down in this room, but like everything else Cynthia had done, it was beyond exquisite.

"Earth calling Dad," Cassandra said, and he realized he hadn't been listening to her.

"Sorry, Cassie, what? Bad signal."

"I asked you what is going on."

For a startled moment, Brad thought Cassandra must be referring to Faith being tucked away at Wolf's Song.

He realized, given their conversation this morning, he did not want Cassie to know anything about the woman in the cottage. Would his daughter take one look at her, and find Faith perfect for him?

He couldn't imagine anything more alarming that Cassandra deciding to play Cupid. For his own good!

Somehow, it seemed impossible that they had just had that conversation this morning. It felt to Brad as if a lifetime had gone by.

"My phone's going crazy," Cassie told him.

Join the club, he thought.

"So is the front desk. Everybody wants to know about the rescue on the lake."

"Oh?" he said innocently. "What rescue?"

"Dad! They're saying you saved a woman and a dog who had gone through the ice on Cobalt Lake."

"Oh. That. It was nothing, really. You know how people love a great story. Remember when the gondola got stuck on Whistler and that ski-patrol woman went up on the ladder and got all those people off? Heroine for a week?"

"Dad! Don't downplay it. It sounds amazing," Cassie said. "And we still have lots of media people in town and hanging around the resort because of Gregor."

Cassie was usually working with security to protect their guests from the media, not approaching them.

"I could not have set up better publicity for the lodge if I tried," she breathed.

He went very still. "Catastrophe is not a publicity opportunity," he said sternly.

"But it wasn't a catastrophe. It was a disaster averted. From what I'm hearing, you prevented something terrible from happening."

"Leave it, Cassie."

He read her silence on the other end of the line as being slightly stunned.

"Dad?"

"Look, I've got a really bad signal. I've got to go."

With the tiniest niggle of guilt, Brad disconnected from Cassie and looked around the room that had been one of Cynthia's pride and joys.

Like the cottages, and the lodge, and even their private residence, this room had been done by a designer.

A very famous and expensive designer who had her own television show on the home-and-garden channel.

Cynthia had needed perfection.

He had felt indulgent of that need. She had come from a working-class background, and especially in the early days of their marriage, he thought she had felt she needed to prove herself to his parents, his mother in particular.

But had Cynthia lost something in that quest for perfection? Something of herself? Is that why he found Faith so compelling. *Real?*

He'd seen the expression on Faith's face when he'd said a designer did Wolf's Song. If he was not mistaken, it had been faintly sympathetic, as if he had missed something.

This room was beautiful by any standard, and yet now, as never before, he could feel it missing something, too.

Cynthia had loved collecting wine. Drinking it? Not so much. She wanted it "to age." Like everything else about her, the cellar was highly organized, with the rarest wines behind glass on the back wall, soft light sweeping down on the temperature-controlled display racks.

The cellar had been mostly for show. Occasionally, she'd hosted a wine afternoon for "the girls," but mostly, she had just collected.

Is that what he had been, too? For show? Where was her heart in this room? In those impeccably designed rooms? Where had her heart been in the marriage?

He hated these questions.

He wasn't indulging them anymore.

He went and inspected the wall that displayed her most valuable collectibles. Now, he saw there were probably five hundred bottles in this section.

If he drank a bottle every week, it would take him ten years to get through it.

Maybe he should break it out for Cassie's wedding—if his independent, fiery daughter ever found a man who was her equal.

Suddenly it felt ridiculous to "age" the wine, to save it for "special" occasions that never came.

They had *really* never come for his wife.

If there was a lesson to be had from Cynthia's premature death, maybe it was that. The time was now.

Still, he hesitated. Was it a special occasion? It felt like it was. But that was a feeling he needed to fight, not give in to.

But he was going back over there, anyway. Faith had to eat. They both did. Why not bring the wine?

It had been a supertough day. He didn't have to drink it with her—he could just present it to her, as a gift.

Feeling like a rebel—and slightly guilty, as well—Brad randomly selected a bottle from the most exclusive shelf and then made his way up to the restaurant kitchen to collect a dinner for two that Anita, the resort's long-time sous-chef, had put together for him.

He stopped at the front desk. "Hey, Kathy, any word about that purse?"

"No, sorry. Jim had a team out there looking, but they didn't find anything. He left a note here for you."

She passed it to him. Brad glanced at it, then shoved it in his pocket.

"He said your voice-mail box was full."

"Actually, while I'm here, I might as well grab a couple of cell phones."

"Of course." She went to a large cabinet where they kept an inventory of things guests might need, everything from toothbrushes to a selection of specialty pillows.

"There you go, Mr. Daniels. I heard what you did—"

He held up his hand. "That's why I need a new cell phone. Suddenly everybody in the whole village and beyond wants to talk to me."

"That explains the full voice mail. The world does love a hero, Mr. Daniels."

100 THE BILLIONAIRE'S FESTIVE REUNION

"Huh," he said. He opened one of the cell-phone boxes.

"This is the number," he told Kathy. "If the police call about that missing purse, you can give it to them. And to Jim, if he finds it. No one else. Am I clear?"

"But Cassandra, of course?"

He was shocked that he wanted to say no, but he didn't. He knew Cassie's phone number. If it came up on the caller ID of the new phone, he could decide then if he wanted to talk to her.

And then he stopped at his office and got rid of his own phone. The number of missed calls and texts was becoming ridiculous. Brad felt a startling sense of freedom as he slid it into his desk drawer. People needed to get lives.

As he walked away, he wondered when the last time was that he'd been without his phone.

It wasn't until he was on his way back over to Wolf's Song that he realized taking some back hallways out of the lodge had paid off. For the first time since she'd been born, he was happy *not* to see his daughter.

CHAPTER NINE

FAITH WAS SO glad she had not been able to find the energy to tell Brad no when he'd gone to get dinner for them.

Because the truth was, as the scents wafted off the containers he had brought back to Wolf's Song, she was suddenly famished.

She did wish, though, that she would have found the energy to go rummage around her suitcase, have a quick shower and throw on some attractive clothes, a bit of makeup.

Because it was the first time she'd seen him without a winter jacket on. He was in a plaid flannel shirt, the plaid in subtle shades of gray, almost identical to his hair. The shirt was open at the column of his throat. With it, he was wearing crisp, khaki mountain slacks, belted at his narrow waist.

Though he had obviously changed since the rescue, he didn't look as if he'd put much effort into it. Even when they were young, she never remembered him fussing over his appearance. And still, Brad Daniels looked front-cover-of-a-men's-outdoor-magazine-worthy.

She couldn't help but notice he'd left his shoes on, was a person who had seemingly never once in his life given a thought to a scratched floor, or puddles.

The *staff* looked after things like that. But she waved the thought away, like a pesky fly that was trying to spoil a perfect moment.

He knew his way around the cottage and refused her offer for help, telling her just to sit at the built-in banquette in an alcove nestled in the windows of the kitchen. He opened the wine he had brought with the efficiency of one who had opened fine wines—as in corked, not screw-top—many times.

He poured a splash in two glasses and set them, and the bottle, on the table, then brought over plates and cutlery, and the boxed food, his movements efficient and comfortable.

She noted the tulip-shaped wineglasses had the unmistakable look of hand-blown crystal. The plates and cutlery had a similar aura—yes, he moved in a world where place settings gave off an aura—of being expensive and exclusive.

Finally, he sat down and lifted his glass to hers, and they clinked, the glasses giving off the crisp note that confirmed their high quality.

"What is this?" she asked, after her first sip of wine. It was a white, which was nice. Red always made her self-conscious about her teeth. Faith was certain she had never tasted a wine quite so lay-ered in delightful, exotic flavors.

"Not sure." He studied the label and shrugged, much as he had when looking at her suitcase.

"Taste it," she suggested.

He took a sip. Unfortunately, it made her very aware of his lips. "Hey, that's pretty good," he decided.

That seemed like an understatement. "Have you ever tasted anything like that before?" she asked.

"Um… I don't know. I'm not much of a wine guy."

"Well, you don't have to be a wine person to know this is unbelievable. It's ambrosia."

Again, that easy shrug, dismissing the fineness of the wine in the same way he had barely noticed her suitcase. Brad served the food. It was a Parmesan-crusted chicken on fettucine noodles. The noodles had so obviously been made from scratch, not been dumped out of a box into boiling water.

It occurred to Faith that maybe, just maybe, the reason why the wine and the food seemed so, so good was that it was all part of that intoxicating feeling she had of coming alive.

And part of that was from being with Brad Daniels. Okay, maybe quite a lot of it!

"So what brought you back to Whistler?" Brad asked. "After all these years? You said you had come here to do something."

The chicken was as exquisite as the wine. "My dad wanted his ashes spread here."

"Oh, Faith, I'm so sorry. I didn't know he'd died."

"How could you know? He didn't live here anymore. He hadn't for a long time. He left after I did. But this is the place he remembered with the most fondness. He worked at all of the top-twenty ski destinations in the world, at one point or another, but this is where he said his heart was. When he was sick, he asked me to bring him back here."

"The loss of your dad and your husband... You must be reeling." His voice was soft with compassion, and that same softness was in his eyes when he gazed at her.

It was hard not to fall into softness, like being invited to try a feather bed after years of sleeping on rocks.

"Dad predeceased Felix by about five years. That's why, when I realized I couldn't check into the hotel, I said I could just go home, and try again another time. I'd already put it off for so long, it felt like another few months couldn't possibly matter." She laughed, a little self-consciously. "My dad was a great believer in signs, and things don't exactly seem to be lining up in my favor."

Except, gazing at Brad over the lip of an exquisite wineglass, that didn't seem exactly true.

She had landed on her feet, sitting here with her teenage sweetheart, eating food and drinking wine that was top-notch, in a five-star environment.

"My dad was actually one of the first ones to notice things might be off with Felix. I had so much going on. Maggie, after finishing up her law degree, and in true Maggie fashion, deciding it would be nothing to get married, have a baby and start her career in a three-year period. Things got so chaotic that I kept putting it off."

Brad's gaze offered her what she had not offered herself. Forgiveness for the fact that life had gotten in the way of such a meaningful task.

"I think it's time, Faith. You're here. You'll regret it if you go back without doing what you came to do."

She nodded. "I think you're right. I'll figure it out."

"I can give you a hand."

"Oh," she said, "really, I've imposed enough."

"Did your dad want some place, specifically?"

"He loved the Feeney's Pass area. He mentioned the viewing point. I'll hike up there tomorrow. I won't need a wallet for that!"

"You're not going up there by yourself at this time of year."

She was taken aback by the firmness in his voice. It sounded like those orders he had snapped at her out on the ice. It reminded her a bit of her daughter, an implication she was some kind of incompetent moron who couldn't be trusted to do things by herself.

Not that her first day in Whistler had actually

proved Maggie wrong. Or done anything to inspire Brad's confidence in her, either.

Still, she had to discourage him from thinking he could just order her around, despite the fact she had accepted his many kindnesses.

"I grew up hiking mountains all over North America," she said quietly. "I'm not worried about Feeney's Pass."

"Well, you should be." There was an edge to his voice. "There's fresh snow up there."

She felt a surge of annoyance, and realized how truly tired she was. Why else would she be so sorely tempted to tell him to mind his own business, when he'd been so good to her? Her irritability probably had more to do with the events of the day catching up with her than Brad. She checked herself.

Then—while busy biting her tongue nearly in half—she looked at him closely. What she saw on his face was distressing.

"Brad?"

"Cynthia died in an avalanche," he said, his voice husky.

"Brad! I'm so sorry." And so glad she had not reacted to her initial annoyance with him.

"She went skiing by herself. At night. She often did. I don't know why."

She heard so much doubt and pain in that confession. It occurred to her, that despite Brad Daniels appearing to have it all, she did not have a corner on suffering. Or insecurities.

"We've implemented a GPS-tracking-device system here because of it, but even so, I'm not comfortable with you going up there by yourself. I hope you'll allow me to go with you."

Suddenly she saw how important this was for him. She could not refuse him this, even as she saw their lives were tangling a little bit more deeply.

"My daughter thinks it's probably illegal," she said. "She thinks I probably need a permit to spread ashes. I don't intend to get one, just so you know."

"Ah," he said, and lifted his wineglass to her, "so we're to be partners in crime."

"No one would have approved more than my dad."

Brad grinned. She had always loved that grin, lopsided and boyish.

"Max was a legend as a lift mechanic, as you know," he said. "That's why I was a little surprised I hadn't heard of him dying. Ski communities are pretty tight."

It meant the world to Faith that Brad not only remembered her father's name, but had also said such a good thing about him.

"His last job was in Switzerland, until he got sick and came home. Well, not home for him. His home was always on the slopes. He had to come to Toronto, because that's where I was.

"He hated the city and then the hospice. I think he had always just thought when his time came, he would lie down on a mountain, and breathe in the fresh air, and that maybe an eagle would soar overhead. I think that's why he extracted the promise from me to let Whistler be his final resting place."

"I didn't know him well, but I always liked him, Faith—everybody did. He was so funny and outgoing."

"Outrageous," she said with a smile. "A true renegade."

"Here's to the renegades," Brad said, and lifted his glass to her father.

At Max's specific request, there had been no funeral. No words spoken. That casual toast by Brad felt so good, so right, so overdue.

They tapped glasses again, and took sips in memory of her father.

"I'm afraid I'm not much of a salute to his legacy," Faith said with a sigh.

"Don't say that. You are!"

She raised an eyebrow at him.

"Not a renegade, obviously," Brad said, "illegal scattering of ashes aside, but I was always so taken with the way you seemed able to be totally yourself, even given—"

He stopped, clearly uncomfortable. He didn't have to say it. *Even given* that she had been living in a trailer, *even given* that she did not have the good clothes, *even given* that she never had lunch money or even money to go for a Coke with the gang after school.

"I know my dad's legend was certainly not all about his mechanical skills," she said dryly.

Brad said, with unmistakable fondness, "Remember him at World Cup?"

"Oh, yeah," she said. Max had somehow gotten himself at the start line, and launched himself down the course on his skis. The timer had gone off automatically as he passed it.

She'd been a spectator, and recognized her father's style and crouch immediately. She had never seen anyone, not even all those pro skiers, dance with powder the way he did. But that day, he had not been dancing. It had been a full-frontal attack.

She'd watched, with her heart in her throat, thinking he was going to be badly hurt. But, no, he had finished the course, straightened and waved his poles with a flourish at the roaring crowd.

"His time," Brad remembered fondly, "was the third best recorded that day. Legend."

"Unofficially. He got arrested for his mischief."

"Did he? I'm sorry, I didn't know that part."

"He said it was worth it," she recalled, with reluctant affection. "I was so mad at him at the time, though! And then it wasn't that long after, in the dead of night, that he scaled one of the lift towers."

"The talk of the town!" Brad said. "Forty feet

in the air, and he managed to get himself off the tower and onto one of the chairs."

"He wasn't nearly as skillful at getting himself back off, and when they found him in the morning, he was nearly frozen."

"But the guy who found him said Max was quite merry, announced he had just been singing his death song to the dawn."

"In Celtic, apparently."

"Legend."

"It wasn't always easy being the legend's daughter," she said.

"I knew that, even then. And yet, you had some of that in you. The sense of humor, the sense of fun. I really did think you stood out from everyone else."

That had been so intoxicatingly evident at the time. And it was true, despite so many insecurities, that she had been fairly certain of who she was. Somewhere along the way, she had lost that certainty.

"It's because he loved me," she told Brad softly. "My dad had flaws, and many of them, but I always knew how much he loved me. I felt utterly cherished by him, and it did give me a sense of myself."

When had she begun rejecting that sense of herself given to her by her father? Perhaps with Mrs. Daniels's cruel assessment of her as not suitable for her son.

CHAPTER TEN

"BUT THEN, almost in reaction to Max's shenanigans, his free spirit, I became the opposite," Faith revealed, finding herself confiding in Brad. "Desperately seeking normal, liking rules and structure."

When she put it like that, it sounded as if she had become *uptight*, as conventional and boring as her father had once predicted she would be.

"And did you get that?" he asked softly, and there was no judgment in his voice.

"Oh, yes. Felix was one of my professors in university. He was quite a bit older than me. He acted as if he didn't know I existed, of course, which was so appropriate.

"That was one of the things I loved about him actually. He was always so concerned about what was appropriate. It was the opposite of what I had grown up with.

"But a year after I'd graduated and was in my first year of teaching, I ran into him in a coffee shop near my school. I found out later it wasn't an accident. He'd looked for me having let a suitable amount of time go by so that it was *appropriate*— and was kind of checking out the coffee shops in my neighborhood.

"He was most worried about our age difference. He was ten years older than me. But it never bothered me at all. A year later we were married." She sighed. "My father proclaimed him dull as porridge."

She shouldn't have said that! She looked at the wine the very same way she had looked at the IV drip earlier.

She glanced at Brad, a man who would never be called that by anyone! It made the words she had just said feel like a betrayal.

"But he wasn't," she said hastily. "I had the life I dreamed of."

There. That was a good note to end on. But somehow, she was still talking, and she was sure the wonderful wine was to blame.

"And then I didn't. And it's kind of left me wondering where all that adherence to the rules got me. My somewhat unpredictable upbringing made me think about every possibility for chaos and disruption, and head it off before it happened. So much energy spent doing that—and all that time the thing I'd least expected, the thing I could not prepare for, was probably already growing in Felix's brain."

"And that's probably why you dashed out on

that lake," Brad said. "Leaving all those fears behind you."

"My dad would have approved of the doggy dash," she said. And it occurred to her that he would have. Not just of her giving in to an impulse, after a lifetime of controlling them, but of everything that had happened after.

Her unexpected reunion with Brad.

The loss of her purse, forcing her to adapt, to accept that the unpredictable was part of life, and that it could be a good part.

Look at where she was!

Something shivered along her spine, almost as if Max was sitting at the table with her, laughing. And then it felt as if she heard his voice.

Don't you love it when a plan comes together?

She really was way too tired. She really could not even have one more sip of that wine. She really could not spend one more moment with Brad. She shivered.

"You're still chilled," Brad said. "Let's move in front of the fire."

She shouldn't. She needed to beg off. To say she was tired, to wish him good-night, to go to bed.

But there was that question again.

All her life of doing everything she *should* do, and where had it gotten her? Since they were going to spend more time together, anyway, why not just surrender?

They moved to the couch in front of the fire,

sitting together on it, nearly shoulder-to-shoulder. His scent was so completely and deliciously clean and male. Somehow, the wineglasses were full again, and he finally took off his shoes, hooking the back of them with his toes and letting them drop to the floor.

He put his feet up on the wooden live-edge coffee table that, from the size of it, must have been made from a thousand-year-old tree.

Faith laughed at his socks, which were bright red with little green monkey faces on them.

"What on earth?" she asked. "You're so cover-of-the-outdoor-gentlemen's-magazine, and then those?"

He wiggled his colorfully clad toes at her.

"Cassie got them for me last year for Christmas. It was her answer to 'what do you get the guy who has everything?' It's a membership to a sock club. They send me a couple of wild and crazy pairs of socks every single month. It seems to just tickle Cassie that I actually wear them, so I do."

Faith loved all the things that told her about Brad's relationship with his daughter. She was aware of feeling a drowsy sort of contentment. It was so much like it had been when they were young. It was easy to be together, the conversation flowing as naturally as a river.

She found herself telling him about the nursery painting disaster, and baking cookies with her grandchildren.

"You know," he said, "I've never baked a cookie."

"Come on."

"No, really, never."

For the second time, Faith felt something like pity for Brad Daniels, the man who seemed to have everything. He'd never painted a nursery the wrong color, never painted at all, in fact. And never baked cookies.

So she told him about some of that, about Maggie and Michael growing up, about the delight of grandchildren, about Maggie becoming a lawyer, and Michael following his heritage back to Scotland to get a doctorate in Scottish history.

"I've worried about how employable that degree will make him."

Brad laughed. "He'll probably end up a professor, like his dad."

She liked it that he seemed to listen so carefully, and that he spoke of Felix with the respect of someone who had not seen, firsthand, the horrible consequences of his illness, and how it had changed the relationships he'd had with everyone who knew him.

She encouraged him to share stories about his daughter, and Faith loved the tenderness and pride in his voice when he talked about her.

They laughed easily together, as they always had.

Somehow, silence descended, and into that silence an aching awareness of him rushed in. Faith glanced at the fullness of his lips.

Memories tickled along her spine.

Brad held her eyes, and then his gaze drifted to her own lips. He reached out with his thumb and scraped her cheek, and then the fullness of her lip. She should have pulled away from that thumb, but she didn't. She leaned into it.

Brad, to his credit, pulled away. He actually looked at his hand as if it was a soldier that had disobeyed a command.

"We're both tired," he said. "It's not the best time to make a decision."

Did that mean he did think the time was coming? To make a decision? About touching each other's lips? And possibly more than that?

He was right.

It was not something to be decided lightly, not something to fall into because they were both beyond exhaustion, in the grip of the dramatic events of the day, and the surprising sweetness of their reunion.

Brad got up off the couch and stretched. It showed off the broadness of his chest, and a rippling of lovely muscles in his arms. His shirt lifted and showed the hard contours of his tummy.

It was breathtaking.

Faith reminded herself, sternly, that her tummy did not have hard contours. Thank goodness, they had backed off on what was developing between them before Brad had made that discovery!

"Oh," he said, "I brought you a phone." He picked it out of his pocket and laid it on the table.

"You just happen to have extra cell phones lying around?"

"It's probably the number-one thing our guests lose or break, particularly during ski season. Supplying loaner phones was one of Cassie's—Cassandra's—ideas, always offering that little extra service to the guests." He chuckled. "In the spring, though, it's a full-time job picking dead cell phones out of melting snow drifts."

"Thank you," she said, not opening the box just yet, and making note of one more example of her indebtedness to him.

She was shocked to see it was nearly midnight. Way too late to call Maggie. It would be 3:00 a.m. in Toronto. Really, was there anything worse than middle-of-the-night phone calls?

She felt a certain guilty relief about that.

"I had to grab a new phone, too," Brad said. "Mine is blowing up. Over the rescue thing."

"Oh, no!"

"I'm doing my best to keep the lid on that."

"Thank you."

"Why don't I come by around ten tomorrow morning, and we'll head up Feeney?"

He was taking charge of everything. She knew she should protest. But she wasn't going to.

"Thank you," she said again. "That sounds perfect."

He hesitated for just a moment. And then he bent, and dropped a quick kiss on her cheek. Completely platonic. Almost European.

"It's so good to see you," he said huskily.

Her silly heart, the one that was supposed to be frozen, had let the fire and his nearness warm it right up.

He slipped his shoes back on and was soon out the front door. She heard him locking it with the keypad. Another small gesture that, like the phone, and the meal, and everything he had done, made her feel intensely taken care of.

It just felt so good not to be the one in charge, to let go.

Faith went into the bedroom. Like the rest of Wolf's Song, the space was opulent, a luxurious symphony of soothing neutral shades and rich textures. The bed was a king. Who needed a bed so large?

She was suddenly so exhausted that it was a huge effort to get her nightgown out of the suitcase and wash her face.

The bathroom had a swimming-pool-size tub in it. There was a chandelier over the tub, hundreds of teardrop-shaped crystals suspended from it, winking with light. In the bathroom!

Finally, back in the bedroom, she pulled back those crisp sheets and climbed into that huge bed.

There was a switch beside the bed to turn off the lights.

She was plunged into the kind of complete darkness that city dwellers tended to forget existed.

The expanse of the bed made her feel small.

And very, very lonely.

When she closed her eyes, instead of falling into deep and exhausted sleep, the events on the lake replayed in her mind's eye. She had a terrible night's sleep, and despite that, Faith found herself awake early. She realized her internal clock was refusing to reset from eastern time.

It was nine o'clock in Toronto. She went out into the main area of the cottage and found where she had left the cell phone on the table. She looked out the windows. It wasn't raining, but it was a gray day in Whistler. The mountaintops were swathed in clouds.

She spent a few minutes figuring out the new phone, and then tapped in Maggie's number.

Unlike yesterday, her daughter picked up the unfamiliar number on the first ring.

"Hi, sweetie."

"Mom! I've been so worried."

Faith thought she'd seen that on a bumper sticker once: Live Long Enough That Your Children Worry About You.

"But I called you and told you I'd lost my phone."

"I tried your hotel, and they said you hadn't checked in!"

Faith had not considered that possibility.

"Can you imagine how that made me feel? So then I tried to call that number back, and I reached a message from a man named Daniel. I told him who I was and asked for a call back. I said it was urgent that I speak to you, but he never called me back. What kind of person is that?"

Faith remembered Brad saying he had put his phone away because of all the calls about the rescue.

"He just didn't have his phone with him."

Her daughter, from a generation that practically had their phones growing out of their hands, harrumphed with disbelief.

"And how would you know that?"

"We had dinner together."

"Daniel could have phoned me when you finished. I said it was urgent."

"His name isn't Daniel, it's Brad, and I'm sure he could figure out a three-hour time difference might not make calling back the best idea."

"But how would he know there was a three-hour time difference?"

Faith could feel Maggie shifting into lawyer mode, and prepared herself for the cross.

"Shockingly, where I'm living now came up in our conversation."

"You never said your friend was a *man*."

"I didn't think it was pertinent."

"Mom, where are you? Are you really in Whistler?"

"What?"

"I'm scared," Maggie said. "I know there's something you're not telling me. I could hear it in your voice, in that message you left. You're vulnerable. And you're a woman of some means. Awful people troll the internet looking for people just like you."

Faith looked around at her beautiful surroundings, and almost laughed out loud. If only her daughter knew she was hanging out with a man who was the least likely to be an internet troll looking to prey on a weakened woman.

"You're right," she confessed, aware already she had no intention of confessing all of it. "I didn't tell you everything. I am in Whistler—of course, I am."

She almost said, "I would never lie to you," but realized an omission could be a lie and there was no way she was going to be telling her daughter about going out on the ice after that dog or anything that had happened after.

"I didn't just lose my phone," she continued carefully. "I lost my whole purse. So I didn't have any ID, which is a requirement for checking into a hotel. My friend, whom I've known since high school, and indeed is a man—*as is half the world's population*—put me up for the night."

"At his house?" Maggie breathed, aghast.

"No, sweetie. At the Cobalt Lake Resort. In a private cottage, like a VIP suite."

There was silence. Faith heard her daughter's fingers tapping away, and knew she was busy fact-checking. There was a reason she was such a good lawyer!

Finally, Maggie spoke.

"Mom," she said, "you know what comes up when I put in Cobalt Lake? Gregor Watson. Is he there right now?"

"Rumors abound," Faith said, tickled that her superpragmatic daughter was just a little bit star-struck.

"It's a gorgeous place. I'm on their website now."

"It's very beautiful," Faith agreed.

"Is it decorated for Christmas? Because it's absolutely spectacular at Christmas."

"Um…not yet." Last night that was one of the things Brad had told her his daughter was working on for the first time since her mother had died.

Her voice a whisper of pure discovery, Maggie said, "Brad Daniels is…"

Faith waited for Maggie to share what she'd found out. That Brad Daniels was the owner of that resort. That he owned quite a lot, actually. That he was most likely a billionaire.

But with all that information at her fingertips, that was not what Maggie said.

She said, "Mom. Brad Daniels is gorgeous."

CHAPTER ELEVEN

HER DAUGHTER'S ASSESSMENT of Brad was fresh in Faith's mind when he knocked lightly on the door and let himself into Wolf's Song.

He *was* absolutely and utterly gorgeous. He was obviously ready for an excursion in the great outdoors, in a down jacket and multipocketed canvas expedition pants. He had on light hikers, so she couldn't see what his sock selection for the day was.

Faith was glad she had freshly showered, done her hair, applied a bit of makeup. She'd chosen her outfit with care—a pair of slacks suitable for a hike, a beautiful white cashmere sweater that maybe was not exactly hiking material.

And she had not chosen the outfit just to send off her father, either.

"Hey," Brad said, "how did you sleep?"

She smiled inwardly. Brad was no more aware of the differences in her hair and makeup, the way she was dressed, than he had been of aware of the quality of the suitcase or that wine he had brought over.

And yet, when he took her in, that smile playing across the beautiful curve of his lips, she felt completely *seen*.

"Restless. I'd forgotten how quiet it is in the mountains. And how dark. You'd think those would lead to a better rest, but I think I missed the noise and light of the big city right outside my window. You?"

"Same. Restless. Had trouble letting go of the events of the day."

His arms were full and he went by her and set a bag and a drink tray with two steaming cups on the kitchen island. He opened the bag and pulled out a selection of croissants and bagels, and little pots of jam and cream cheese.

"That smells heavenly."

"Still take it black?" he asked her, passing her one of the cardboard cups.

Who remembered how you took your coffee after thirty some years?

"Yes. You're spoiling me."

He met her gaze. "You know what? You deserve some spoiling."

It should have made her feel as if she had confided too much in him, and had earned his pity, but that's not how she felt, and it was not pity she saw in his eyes.

It was such genuine caring it took her breath away. She went over and took the coffee he offered.

"Do you still take two creams and a sugar?"

she asked him. Ridiculous to feel as if that was flirting.

But his grin told her he found it endearing that she remembered, too.

"You want the good news or the bad news?" he asked her.

"Good, of course."

"There isn't any."

She laughed and blew on her coffee.

"The staff searched around the lake extensively. No purse. I checked with the police first thing this morning, and no purse had been turned in there yet, either."

She considered the logistics of that. How was she going to begin the process of replacing at least enough things to get her home?

"Also, it's not a perfect day for going up Feeney. It's not snowing or raining, but it could start. It's cold and damp out there. You're still okay to go?"

"Yes." Considering she had put off this task for so long, it now felt weirdly imperative that she do it.

"You can add to this morning's list of *not-so-good news* that my daughter is very annoyed with me."

"Hey!" he said. "Mine, too."

And they bumped their coffee cups, in silent congratulation for achieving the goal of having become an irritation to their children.

"It never occurred to me Maggie would call

the hotel to try and track me down. I'm afraid the next time you check your messages on your other phone, you'll find a few from her."

"That's too bad that she worried."

"Takes after her mother more than she cares to admit."

Brad smiled at Faith, as if the worry gene was adorable. Then reached into a front shirt pocket and put a card down on the table.

"What is that?"

"It's a preloaded credit card."

"I can't take that!"

"What are you going to do then? Call me every time you want a cup of coffee?"

"That's a good point." His thoughtfulness was so compelling. "I'll pay you back as soon as I have access to funds, though."

He lifted a shoulder, clearly uncaring of whether or not she paid him back.

"I came on a quad," he said, referring to the four-wheeled all-terrain vehicles that were commonly used in the mountains before there was enough snow to bring out the snowmobiles.

"I wasn't sure if you'd prefer that to hiking, since the weather isn't that good?"

"Oh, I'd love that!"

"I'm glad you said that, because I wasn't sure about going as far as the viewing point on foot if it's going to snow."

"I haven't been on a quad since I left here."

"Really?"

"I'm afraid for the last thirty or so years experiencing the great outdoors meant taking a book and a picnic to St. James Park on a sunny afternoon."

Felix had been *not outdoorsy*, and not the least apologetic about that, either. Once, she had talked him into a camping trip with the kids. It had been a fiasco from beginning to end: mosquitos, poor-quality sleeping bags that had left them cold and the hotdogs burned to the point of being inedible over the campfire.

Startled, Faith realized that, little by little, she had surrendered her own interests to Felix.

But isn't that part of why she was here?

Not just to honor her father's last wish, but to discover some lost part of herself? The part of her father that was deeply ingrained inside her? Outdoors. Adventure. Challenges.

"Actually, I can't wait to get back on a quad," she said.

"We can get you your own, or you can ride with me."

"I don't know if after so long I'd be confident riding one solo, especially up the steep parts of that pass."

There was some truth to that, but even more truth to the irresistible nature of sharing the seat of a quad with him.

An hour later, Maggie would have been shocked to see her mother, in her puffy new parka, sitting astride a quad, her arms wrapped tightly around this fabulously good-looking man.

Faith had her nose buried in Brad's rather gorgeous shoulder as they traversed the rocky, steep trail.

A box of ashes, in a velvet drawstring sack, was on her lap, squished tightly between them, and that was all that prevented Faith from being pressed even more intimately into Brad Daniels.

She was glad for the warm coat Brad had provided her with the day before, and for the fact he had given her gloves, as well. It really was a cold morning.

She was also very glad she had left the driving to him. Despite the thick, cold mist, every now and then she would catch a heart-stopping glance of the steep drop-offs beside the trail.

Soon, the warmth radiating off Brad and the pureness of her surroundings edged out the chill.

It was replaced with a sense of exhilaration, almost homecoming, as they headed into places so high and wild that few people ever got to experience them. The moist morning air was scented heavily with pine and cedar.

The quad was quite quiet, humming along the difficult trail, instead of growling.

As Brad guided the vehicle confidently over the steadily increasing steepness of the rugged trail, the grayness around them began to thin, as did the trees.

Faith realized what had seemed like cold fog was actually a cloud. And then they drove right through it, and came out on top of it, into dazzling sunshine and a bright blue sky.

They were just a few feet from the viewing point, which looked out over the steep valley that separated some of the most majestic peaks of the Fitzsimmons Range of the Coast Mountains.

Brad stopped the quad.

Even though it had not been very noisy, once the sound of the engine was gone, the silence of the mountains and the forest below them was immense. Faith slipped off her perch behind him, resting her precious cargo on the seat while she took off her helmet.

Then she picked it up her father's ashes, hugging that humble velvet bag to her. She walked to what seemed to be the edge of the earth.

She had forgotten how sacred these high places felt, the air beyond pure, the world swathed in clouds below them, the snowcapped, formidable mountain peaks marching off into infinity around them.

Brad came and stood beside her.

"Do you want to be by yourself?"

"No, actually, I think he'd like it that you were here. He liked you."

She took a deep breath. Her fingers, despite the gloves, were cold. They trembled on the drawstrings.

Without asking, Brad—just knowing what needed to be done—helped her with the strings, and then held the sides of the bag, peeling it back as Faith pulled out the plain white cardboard box that was inside.

She wondered if she should tell Brad this humble container was her father's wish, not hers.

But a glance at his face told her he was no more aware of the humbleness of the container than he had been of her suitcase.

In the hospice, Max had handed her an envelope thick with cash.

"This is to pay for it. A cremation. Don't put me in the ground," he'd insisted. "And don't let them talk you into any of their scammy stuff, funeral-home nonsense—fancy urns, and stupid cards with pictures on them. There's enough there to do it simple and to take me back to the high places."

"Dad! You don't have to pay for it yourself."

"Oh, Faith, what would I do with money where I'm going?"

She couldn't argue with that.

"It's the least I can do. You know, I never forgave myself for betting your college money."

"I know, Dad. We don't have to talk about it—"

"You let me say my piece. The worst of it was I played right into that wicked witch's hands."

"What wicked witch?" she'd asked, stunned.

He snorted. "I knew Deirdre Daniels couldn't stand it that her son loved you."

"I had no idea that you knew about Brad and me."

"I might not be great at playing the horses, but I was always good at reading people. I knew what was going on between you and the Daniels kid. I liked him. More evidence, as if I needed it, that rotten parents can have good kids."

His gaze had rested on her a little too long.

"You weren't a rotten parent!" she'd said.

"I gambled away your college money."

"Oh, Dad, everything worked out in the end. It's not as if Brad and I were going to go on and get married and have kids. Neither of us was ready for that. I was seventeen, for Pete's sake, he was eighteen. I've been happy with Felix. I wouldn't have changed a thing."

Again, his eyes had been on her face, so direct. He'd hesitated.

"You know there's something wrong with the old guy, eh?"

She hated it that he always called Felix that. "Wh-wh-what?" she had stammered.

"When was I here last?"

"Two years ago, at Christmas."

"Oh, yeah, that's right. The year I worked at Schweitzer. That's a good hill. You should go there sometime. Take Maggie and Michael. It's in Idaho."

He hadn't said it with recrimination, but she was pretty sure it bothered him that his grandchildren didn't ski, hadn't experienced the high places.

"You're not noticing," Max had said, his voice a tired whisper, "because it's probably happening slowly. But for me, not having seen the old guy for two years, the changes can't be denied. Can't miss them. I'm tired, pet. Maybe you can come back tomorrow."

But there had been no tomorrow.

And then she *had* seen the changes. Once she did start seeing them, she was not sure how she had missed them. Maybe because of a full life: graduations, a marriage and babies, her dad's illness, work.

But after Max had passed, it had been like there were alarm bells clanging in her head, accompanied by red and white flashing lights.

Felix's curious lack of affect about the death of her dad, and then about the birth of Maggie's baby, their first grandchild.

His increasingly insensitive and inappropriate remarks.

How could she have not noticed Felix, of all people, being inappropriate?

He started being mean. Last Christmas, after he complained childishly about the turkey being dry, he shook his head sadly at Maggie, and said, "I never thought I'd have a fat daughter."

Michael, who had traveled all that way to be with them, had set down his cutlery quietly, and said, "I've had about enough of you sniping at Mom and Maggie. You've been doing it since I got here."

In a blink, Felix had been out of his chair, towering over the seated Michael, his fists clenched. "What are you going to do about it then?"

Faith had had the shocking feeling that they were about to become *that* family, the one where the police arrived at their house on Christmas day.

The exact kind of family she had seen in Deirdre Daniels's judgment of her all those years ago, that she had spent her whole life trying to outrun.

"Are you okay?" Brad asked her now.

Was she okay? Her father had noticed the changes in her husband long before she had, but he had probably noticed the toll those changes were taking on Faith, too. Even before Felix's illness, Max had thought she was giving up parts of herself.

Was that why he had sent her on this mission back to Whistler?

To let him go?

But to find herself, too?

CHAPTER TWELVE

"I'M OKAY," Faith reassured Brad with a nod.

And then, she opened the box. She had not opened it before. Inside it was a thick, clear plastic bag, fastened with one of those impossible zip ties.

Without saying a word, Brad slipped a knife from one of those many pockets in his mountaineer pants. As cosmopolitan as he was, he had been born and raised traversing these backcountry trials. He would no more be caught in the wild places without a knife than he would be caught without water.

He slit the top of the bag open, and then he stepped back and behind her.

She was aware it was a physical gesture, but it felt symbolic, too. Brad had her back.

She lifted the bag up and away from herself. Slowly, she tilted it upside down. Some of the ash was light, like dust, and hung in the air, floated upward, suspended, almost glittering in the strong sunlight.

Some was picked up by the breeze and carried away.

And some fell into rocky crevasses and onto rugged outcrops. As she shook the last of her father's ashes from the bag, there was an incredible sense of relief, of rightness, of peace.

As if Max was finally home.

"Look," Brad said quietly.

And then from behind her, he put his arms around her waist, and she leaned back into him and tilted her head up to look at the intense blue of the sky.

Together, they watched as the bald eagle, possibly the largest one she had ever seen, danced and soared on the wind currents above them.

"In the end," she said softly, "this is what was left of a man."

"No," Brad said. "You're what's left of the man, Faith. You're his legacy. And you're a good one."

So it was not just her father who had come home.

With Brad's arms around her, and his voice stirring her hair, Faith felt she had come home, too.

She had expected she might cry when she let go of Max this final time. Instead, she felt a sense of closure, and having done right by her father.

He would have *loved* this.

Instead of feeling devastated by fresh grief, Faith felt an unexpected sense of euphoria and release as she silently wished Max well on his journey, and thanked him for all the gifts he had given her.

Among the best of them: to embrace the moment in all its unpredictability, to embrace the unexpected joys life gave you.

Brad contemplated how deliciously right it felt to be here on the mountaintop with Faith. It felt like such a grave honor to be trusted to help her with this most sacred of responsibilities.

"Do you feel the way I feel?" he asked her, finally releasing her. The eagle had vanished, riding a wind current up and up and up, until it was but a speck in the sky and then they couldn't see it at all.

She turned and looked at him. "Like a part of something bigger than us all?"

"Exactly," he breathed.

"Yes, I do. I feel at peace. And oddly happy."

"Exactly as Max would have wanted," Brad said. He felt oddly happy, too. To be with her, to be in the mountains, to feel such intense connection to all things.

He flattened the now-empty box and stowed it in the pannier of the quad. He saw her tuck the velvet bag inside her jacket, next to her heart.

"Do you feel ready for a hot drink? I brought a thermos with hot chocolate."

"You're spoiling me," she said again.

"I know," he said. "I like it."

Her eyes misted up. She was a woman who had not been spoiled nearly enough. At least not for a long time.

"Maybe not just yet."

Her eyes drifted to the trail, not the way they had been, but where it began to twist downward on the other side of the pass.

"Should we keep going then?" Brad asked. "We can see if we can get as far as the Mud Puddle, or if there's snow that will turn us back before we make it there."

The locals had created a tiny but beautiful rock pool around a hot springs that bubbled naturally out of the rocky earth around it. The water flowed in and out of that pool constantly, making it pristinely clean. Where it sloshed over the rock walls, it had created a decadently warmed mud bath, worthy of any spa.

It was probably the best-kept secret in all of Whistler. The locals did not tell. Anyone. Ever. It was code named the Mud Puddle, so that casual reference to it did not give away the fact there was an extraordinary secret up there in Feeney's Pass.

Some longing flashed through her eyes.

What was he doing, exactly? It felt like something more than just trying to draw that carefree part of Faith back to the surface.

"I can't," she said.

Thank goodness, Brad thought, that Faith was intent on being the reasonable one.

Still, he heard the reluctance in her voice.

"Why not?" he asked, pressing her.

She sighed heavily. "I have to start figuring out

how I'm going to get on my flight on Friday if my purse isn't found. I'm sure there's an overwhelming amount of phone calls that have to be made and paperwork that has to be done."

There. Get back on the quad, and fight all the things his arms wrapped so tightly around her were causing him to feel, and drop her off to do her tasks.

It would be the safest thing.

Safe. Not the choice that would honor her devil-may-care dad.

And yet, he could not miss the longing in her eyes as her gaze drifted again, not to the trail the way they had come, but the other way. To where it went.

He saw how she had carried the weight of the whole world on her shoulders for so long. "You can leave all the responsibilities behind. Just for today."

He had, after all. He'd sent Cassie a quick text this morning, from the new phone, telling her he would be out of cell range for the whole day.

"Nothing would please Max more than that," Faith said pensively, mirroring the thought Brad had just had.

It wasn't quite a yes. He nudged. "Do you want me to see if we get cell service here? I can call the resort and have someone start doing the leg-work about getting on a commercial flight without documents."

"No, don't bother with the cell."

He was relieved by that because he was sure if he opened that new phone there would be a dozen messages from Cassie.

"Come to that, I'm sure Maggie is all over it, already."

"There's another option, too. I can get you home, Faith. I have a plane."

She looked at him, startled. "It's a long way in a small plane, especially at this time of year."

"Uh, it's not a small plane. It's, um, a jet." He needed her to know he was problem-solving, not boasting. "I mean I have access to a jet, I don't own one."

But then that felt dishonest, as if he was trying to downplay himself, and he was aware of wanting one-hundred-percent honesty between them.

"I probably would own one," he confessed, "except that my environmentally sensitive daughter would disown me for the hypocrisy of asking our guests not to have their sheets washed every day, while I'm indulging myself for the sake of convenience. She might say male ego."

To his relief, Faith laughed.

"Our daughters," she said, with a shake of her head. "Why are they so hard to please?"

"Because we raised them to not be afraid to have their own opinions," he said.

"True." And then she added, "And don't worry about the private jet! That hydrogen-fuel technology will probably be applicable to planes someday."

And the best possible thing happened.

They were laughing.

"What's one more day?" Faith said. "I'm sure I'll get home one way or another. Yes, let's see if we can get to the Mud Puddle."

He surreptitiously turned off the tracker that was clipped on to his jacket. Somehow, he did not want his daughter, unable to get him on his phone, looking at a GPS map, watching the little red dot that was him move closer and closer to the Mud Puddle.

It would just lead her to asking too many questions. Questions he was not in any way ready to answer.

He wasn't even sure if he had an answer, beyond following an impulse, and what kind of answer was that?

Faith got back on the quad behind him. The box that had provided some separation on the way up to the viewing point was gone.

Every bump and every rock brought her into closer contact with him. He could feel how snugly he fit between the V of her legs. He could feel her curves, even through the pillowy shape of the jacket she wore.

He could feel her heat.

And her heat seared him.

It filled him with something he had not felt for a very long time.

This was way more than an impulse. It was a

wanting, raw and powerful, like a man who had crawled across the desert wanted water, or like a man who had not slept for weeks wanted to lay himself down, close his eyes and be taken by the abyss.

The snow, thankfully, blocked the trail before they reached the Mud Puddle, which would bring a lot more challenges to his impulses that he was not quite ready for.

They got off the quad.

The moment he was out of close contact with her, it felt—thankfully—as if the spell had been broken.

"End of the line," he declared.

Faith took off her helmet, ran her fingers through her messy hair. The spell threatened to curl around him again, like wisps of smoke coming up from a fire.

"It's not much farther, is it?"

"No, but it'll be slippery."

"Should we try it on foot?"

He cast an experienced glance at the trail. The snow was not deep enough to worry about avalanches, and yet, he felt that reluctance to give himself to the wild places that had so betrayed him.

"I didn't really come prepared for that. I didn't bring towels…or bathing suits."

His eyes met hers. She cocked her head and looked at him. She did not seem like the vulnerable woman who needed his protection. She seemed to know exactly where this could lead.

And what she wanted.

Of course, she had wanted to rescue that dog, too, which showed her decision-making skills might not be the best...

"Maybe it's not—"

"I can't believe you let me down like this, Brad. You've rescued me, you've fed me, you've given me a place to stay and money. You've offered to help me get home, but now this. You've forgotten the bathing suits."

She was teasing him. If felt wonderful. She smirked when he got it.

"Okay," he said, "turning in my Boy Scout hero badge. A bit of a relief, I must say."

"My dad used to say the Puddle was a healing place. That even the animals knew. That a sick animal would go lie down in the heated mud. I can't imagine being this close and not going there. What do you think?"

What he thought was alarming. He was not sure he could refuse Faith anything.

"Sure," Brad said. "We don't actually have to get in. Maybe just stick our feet in the mud."

"Does that make you a stick-in-the-mud, Brad?"

Was she suggesting she wanted to do more than stick her feet in the mud? His face felt suddenly hot.

"Am I remembering wrong?" Faith asked. "I

don't remember anyone wearing bathing suits in the Mud Puddle, because the mud just wrecked them, anyway."

No, she was remembering that with one-hundred-percent accuracy. Was she actually trying to make him blush?

What else was she remembering? Because he was remembering youthful exuberance, laughter, both of them being kind of shy and kind of bold, the slipperiness of the mud, kisses hotter than that sulfur-scented water.

She rummaged around in the pannier and pulled out the thermos. He found a couple of bottles of water. With her free hand, she took his free hand, as if that was the most natural thing in the world. They began to make their way up the slippery trail.

They pushed and pulled and clawed through the snow, and over the icy patches, until they arrived at their destination, breathless.

Brad was pleasantly surprised by how this, his first venture into this kind of country in a long, long time, did not feel anxiety-provoking.

The opposite.

He felt his soul soothed by the pristine atmosphere of the high alpine, where the Mud Puddle was located, well above the tree line. Its smell—strong and sulfury—like rotten eggs, alerted them to how close they were before they actually saw it.

It was tucked behind a wall of rocks, well off

Feeney's Pass, which was probably why the locals had succeeded in keeping it a secret so long. The slightly beaten path to it could have been mistaken for an animal trail, and indeed, there were some animal footprints in the snow, but no sign of human activity.

Brad watched Faith's face as they squeezed through the tiny little opening in the rocks and found themselves in an open area on the other side, a breathtaking view of the mountains around them.

"You know how some things aren't quite as you remembered them?" she breathed.

"Yes."

"This is better than I remembered it." She sat down on an outcropping and removed her light hikers and socks. She rolled up her pant legs and then sank her feet into the mud.

"Oh, my," she said and made a sound in her throat of deep and sensual pleasure. Then she opened her eyes and looked at him. "This isn't going to be good enough," she told him solemnly. "I can't come all the way here, and not get in. I would regret it forever."

CHAPTER THIRTEEN

BRAD QUESTIONED IF he had ever really thought they were going to get up here and just be satisfied to soak their feet and drink hot chocolate.

Twenty-four hours ago he certainly could not have predicted being at the Mud Puddle with Faith Cameron. Saint-John.

In fact, everything about his life with Cynthia had been ordered. Predictable. If you had asked him, he would have said he liked it that way.

But then the way she had died... Who could have predicted that? It was as if it was in total defiance of her own highly structured life.

He thought of that eagle soaring on the updraft, just letting life take it.

Live, something whispered to him. *Live*.

He took off his jacket and cast it aside. Now what?

She was looking at him to show the way. He could see it in her eyes, that she was wrestling with the insecurity of not being young anymore. Neither of them were young anymore. And they had both probably seen plenty of bodies in various circumstances.

"We can pretend we're Icelandic," she said, but her uncertainty was endearing. "That whole country is covered in hot springs. I don't think anyone worries about bathing suits."

"I've been there. On business. They're global leaders in geothermal technology. You're right about there being hot springs everywhere. Almost every town, even ones so tiny you wouldn't expect it, has a pool heated geothermally. But everywhere I went, people had on bathing suits."

"Oh," she said. "Did you go to the Blue Lagoon?"

"Yes. It's amazing. There are pockets of white mud in it, called silica, that you smear all over your bathing-suit-clad body."

She laughed. "It's on my bucket list. What's on yours?"

He'd lived an extraordinary life, he realized, where if he wanted to do anything, he had always been able to make it a reality.

He was surprised to hear himself reveal something. "I hope someday I'll be painting a nursery for Cassie."

He realized she was looking to him for leadership. He took a deep breath and stripped to his shorts.

The mountain air bit into his skin. He tried to keep his eyes to himself as beside him Faith peeled off item after item of clothing, until she was in her underwear, too.

"It's no different than being at the beach," she said bravely.

"Exactly."

"Except I haven't worn a two-piece since my first baby. So don't look!"

He tried hard not to look. Despite the fact they were barely dressed, Brad felt oddly comfortable with Faith, as if they had been married for a hundred years, as if being like this together was as natural as those springs bubbling out of the earth.

His hand found Faith's once again, and together they went to the edge of the pool.

It felt closer to the very edge of the earth than they had been at the Feeney's Pass viewing point.

"The silica in the Blue Lagoon can't have anything on this," Faith said, sliding down into the mud, until she was completely prone, letting its delicious warmth ooze over her body.

She was grateful that this morning, after just a moment's hesitation, she had chosen the underwear he had given her yesterday, unable to resist how pretty it was in comparison to the utilitarian offerings in her own suitcase.

Funny, how what a woman had on, where no one could see it, could make her feel pretty.

Sexy.

Of course, now he could see it, but he was being a perfect gentleman and not looking at her at all.

She scooped up handfuls of mud. It was going to wreck the underwear beyond repair, but she could buy new things. Things more delicate and feminine. Maybe she'd even use that credit card he had given her and check out the Cobalt Lake Boutique before she went home.

She gave herself more completely to the mud, and covered herself thoroughly, partly shy and partly because the warmth of it was so compelling.

She contemplated the fact that with all her imperfections, here she was, nearly naked, in a very sensual setting, with the very gorgeous Brad Daniels.

What would her children think if they knew that after a less-than-twenty-four-hour reunion, she was frolicking in the mud, in her rather sexy undergarments, with her old high-school lover?

Faith decided, firmly, she would not go there. She had long been captive to what other people thought and she would not give away one second of this experience to the imagined recriminations of others.

She had played it safe her entire life.

Where had that gotten her?

She was so tired of being the responsible one. Setting the example, being so damn *good* all the time.

Objectively, she and Brad were just two mature

people giving themselves over to enjoying an unexpected experience.

She slid a glance over at Brad. He had stepped out in the mud, sinking in to his ankles. His broad back was to her. He had on boxer briefs, and was choosing not to lie down, but was standing, bending, cupping his hands in the mud and pouring it—it had the consistency of thick gravy—over himself.

It didn't really feel *racy* being in their underwear together. They were both now also clad, from the tips of their toes to the tops of their heads, with brownish-gray mud.

He looked like the clay form that they cast bronze around. And he was beautiful enough to be replicated into a statue.

Brad was a perfectly made man. Age had not diminished that. If anything, he seemed to have come even more into himself. Broader. More solid, with his long legs, wide shoulders, deep chest, taut belly. Even clothed as he was in mud, she could see the dimples above the band of his shorts, at the small of his back. The little indents were just above the lovely cut of lean buttocks that showed quite clearly through his mud-plastered shorts. Faith was surprised by how clearly she remembered that feature.

She had loved those dimples then. It had felt like a wonderful little secret she knew about him.

Her sense of delight seemed undiminished by a very long hiatus!

Should she feel guilty? What was there to feel guilty about? It wasn't as if she had to submit a report to her children or to anyone else.

It struck her, in a way that it had not before, that she was free. To do and be whatever she wanted.

And at the moment, she was delighted to discover a sense of the mischievous in herself. When was the last time she had been playful, if her grandchildren had not been involved?

Even then, because of the stress of Felix, sometimes it had felt as if she was just going through the motions, playing the role of cheery granny, but not feeling it. At all. Her mind always elsewhere, her heart always numb.

She raised herself on her elbows, picked up a fistful of mud and tossed, aiming toward one of those dimples above his backside. It landed with a satisfying splat, square on one of his broad shoulders.

He turned and gave her a narrow look. At first, she thought he clearly expected more maturity, but then, she saw him gathering his own great fistful of mud.

"Prepare for a muck smush," he said, and stalked toward her, his expression theatrically menacing.

Laughing, she tried to get up, but the mud held her captive. She tried harder and then, with a great slurp, the mud released her and she moved to dash out of his reach. But it was impossible to build any speed with the mud sucking on her feet.

His hand found the middle of her back, and he gleefully ground mud into it. She bent to swiftly reload with a mud missile. When she turned around, he was already sloshing away, throwing taunts over his shoulder.

And just like that, she and Brad were playing like the children they had once been.

Sliding, shrieking, throwing mud balls. Soon, not an inch of skin was visible on either of them. Their hair was caked with mud. Her belly actually hurt from laughing.

He had just dodged her again, and with the mud dripping off him in twisted ropes, he looked like a mythical, hairy beast.

"You're the Sasquatch people claim to see in this area!"

"It's true," he confessed. "My mud-wrestling name in Sasquatch Sam."

"And here's me without my phone! That's a million-dollar photo right there."

"Absolutely not! I protect you from publicity, you protect me and my true identity."

It was pure silliness, and she welcomed it like parched earth welcomed rain.

She closed in on him again, arm raised to slam him with mud, but then when he pivoted to run, his feet skidded out from underneath him, and he was down, sliding through the mud on his butt.

Chortling, she lunged after him, and hovered over him. She was going to get him right in the face.

"Have mercy," he cried. "Man down."

"There is no mercy from the world-famous mud-wrestler, Greta the Barbarian. Prepare for annihilation."

He drew in a deep breath and closed his eyes, as if he was a warrior surrendering to his fate.

Faith chuckled and cried, "Victory!"

But before it was a complete victory, an unbelievably strong hand snaked around her ankle. When she tried to kick free of it, her balance tilted, then tottered, and then she was falling, their mud-slicked bodies coming together with a dull smack.

She was sprawled on top of the whole length of him. The mud-slicked underwear was a poor barrier, indeed. They might as well have both been naked. Slipping and sliding against each other, Faith thought it might have been the most sensual thing she had ever felt.

Only the whites of their eyes showed as they stared at each other, creatures from the deep, warm mud oozing out from between where their bodies were pressed together.

"Greta, I surrender," he whispered.

She freed an arm from between them, and with her thumb, cleared the mud off his lips. But before she could claim them, he slipped out from underneath her, stood and held his hand out to her.

Hand in hand, they walked to the small, rocked-off pool. He helped her slide in, then went and retrieved the thermos. She ducked under the water, and felt the mud melt off her hair and body.

He came, set down the thermos on the ledge and then slid into the pool beside her. He ducked under the water and came up restored to himself. The pool was tiny, with only one way to sit in it, side by side, and shoulder-to-shoulder.

After their dunk, the water turned the same color as the hot chocolate that he'd poured.

But, because it was constantly fed from the spring, it slowly cleared.

Utterly content, they sat on a ledge within the rock pool, water up to their chins, naked shoulders touching, stinky steam rising around them, sipping their hot chocolate.

"I needed that," he said, smiling at her, his dark eyes dancing with merriment. "To laugh like that. To let go."

"Me, too. I can't tell you how much."

"You don't have to. I get it."

And Faith suspected he was the one person on the planet who did get it, entirely. How sorrow was a cloud you walked under, thinking it would never break. That you would never see the sun again.

And yet, right now, both literally and figuratively, she could feel the sun again. She lifted her chin to it and closed her eyes.

CHAPTER FOURTEEN

"CAN I ASK you something?" Brad said to Faith, after a long comfortable silence.

"Or course."

"I've always wondered," he said, and she could hear the caution in his voice, so at odds with the carefreeness they had just experienced, "what happened all those years ago. One minute, we were like this—" he motioned at the pond and the mountains, a gesture that included them "—and the next you were gone."

What was the point, after all these years, of throwing anyone under the bus? Her father's terrible error in judgment, his mother's ability to pounce on an opportunity to control the unfolding of her son's life?

"The money for school just dried up," she said, her tone as careful as his.

"But why didn't you tell me that? I could have helped."

Over his mother's dead body.

But, of course, Mrs. Daniels was dead. There was no sense sullying her memory now.

"I was embarrassed," she said, "and scared."
That was so true.

"But what happened? You just disappeared."

She hesitated. "A benefactor came along and
tossed me a life rope. A full scholarship at U of
T. It was a once-in-a-lifetime thing, and I had to
make some hard decisions really fast."

"I still don't understand why you cut off contact so completely. Not a phone call, or a letter.
Not even a Christmas card?"

*Because Mrs. Daniels had made the terms
abundantly clear.*

"Brad, it's a long time ago."

She didn't realize her brow had furrowed until
he pressed his thumb gently into it.

"Yes, it is," he agreed. But she could see the
pain in his eyes.

"I'm sorry if I hurt you. I really am."

"That's part of what I couldn't understand," he
said quietly. "It seemed so unlike you. To hurt
anyone."

"I'm sorry," she said again.

He looked at her, deeply, as deeply as anyone
had looked at her for a long, long time. It felt as
if he could see the *truth* of her, even though most
days—though not today—she felt she didn't know
that about herself.

"I thought you loved me," he whispered. "As
much as I loved you."

I did, she said silently.

Out loud, she said, "Brad, I was seventeen. You were eighteen. So young. I don't think we realize how young that is until we have our own children, and watch them hit those milestones. How would you have felt if it was your daughter, making decisions that could alter the course of her whole life based on that fierce, unflinching first love?"

"That's true," he said with a sigh. "I felt like she was a baby at seventeen. Sometimes, I still do. But you have a good point. Still, I feel as if there's something you're not telling me."

"Let's just leave it," she suggested quietly, though part of her wanted to trust him with all of it.

Brad sighed.

"You're right. Let's leave it. It's all a long time ago."

There was simply no point in saying to him *My dad gambled away my college money, and your mother was waiting like a vulture to pick over the bones of our lives.*

She had said to her father, on his deathbed, that it had all worked out. And yet, she was aware, in this moment, that didn't mean she didn't feel a residue of resentment around it.

But she didn't need to influence Brad's vision of the world, and his family, by sharing that with him.

For a while, the deep silence of the mountains was comfortable between them.

"Did you have other plans for your stay in Whistler?" he asked her.

She smiled. "I was going to go have dinner at the Mountain Hideaway where my dad would have never been welcomed. And tomorrow I was going to hit some of the shops and buy a few things he would have never been able to afford."

Because, she remembered sadly, Max was saving for her college, a noble gesture that he had spoiled with one impulsive decision. The worst of it was not his decision, but his guilt. He'd put walls around himself, imprisoning him in ways he had never allowed himself to be imprisoned before.

"I guess I was going to kind of thumb my nose at Whistler for Max Cameron. But now, I won't."

"If it's because of funds—"

She held up her hand. "It's not. It's not because of the lost purse. I'm pretty sure that credit card you gave me would cover even a breathtakingly expensive dinner at the Hideaway. But sitting here, where the world is so pure, and so wild, and so free, I don't want to do those things anymore.

"It feels almost as if it would dishonor him. If there was one thing my dad was not, it was into the *show*. To him—" Faith swept her arm over the views all around them, much like Brad had done earlier "—this was true wealth. Living fully. Experiencing creation deeply."

"Maybe it's just as well not to have dinner at the most well-known place in town given the interest of the media in locating the damsel in distress, the hero and the dog."

"Just tell them your hero badge had been revoked, remember?"

"If only it were that easy. They're hounds and the fox is their story. I don't think decency or sensitivity is part of their world."

"Thank you for being decent and sensitive in a world that isn't, Brad."

His hand found hers, and squeezed. She felt the length of his leg touch hers through the heat of the water. She felt a jolt of primal hunger go through her that was both alluring and alarming.

She stroked his leg. In response, he turned to her, gazed at her for a moment and then dropped his lips, nuzzling her neck before pulling away.

"I'm sorry. It just feels so much the way it always felt with you. As if you are steel and I am a magnet, helpless against your pull.

"Don't be sorry," she whispered, stunned—but delighted—that he still found her as attractive as he once had.

Brad's lips on her neck had awakened her awareness that there was a need inside her, not just to be seen as attractive, but to be a woman again. To feel a deep awareness of her own body, to feel that rush of desire, that exquisite moment of fulfilment.

To feel the tenderness of a man's lips, the rasp

of his voice, the worship of his hands, the power of his need.

To experience physical intimacy.

All those things suggested hope for life.

Faith felt the enchantment of the world she found herself in—more, she felt healing blossoming inside of her.

Some barrier—some adherence to the rules she had followed her entire life—dissolved inside Faith with all the resistance of sugar meeting hot water.

"If it's too fast," he told her, "we can slow it down. We don't have to—"

But she put her hand behind Brad's head and drew his lips down to her own, and silenced him. His lips were so soft and so beautiful.

How was it possible to remember a sensation this accurately? And yet, she did—she remembered exactly what it had been like to be with him. And, at the very same time, as the kiss deepened, it felt brand-new and exquisitely exciting.

Her hands explored the water-slicked silk of his heated chest. His belly. She reveled in his hard lines. In letting her hands *know* him.

"Faith," he whispered huskily, "do you know where this is going?"

"Oh, yes."

"Are you sure?"

She laughed against the delicious column of his

throat, nibbled it and then reached up and nipped his ear.

"Of course, I'm sure. It's not as if I can get pregnant."

"I was hoping," he growled against her ear, "it was because you found me completely irresistible."

"Ah, yes, and that."

And then they were laughing together, but the laughter was heated and breathless. He lifted her with astonishing and easy strength, setting her on a rock shelf as he stood before her.

Brad reached behind her, and his hands found the snap on the bra. It fell away, and his eyes drank her in.

Not seeing imperfections at all.

She found the band of those lacy panties, and both of them tugged them off. He stepped out of his shorts.

Faith did not feel self-conscious as his hands took ownership of her, as his eyes worshipped her, as his voice anointed her with blessings.

She wrapped her arms around his neck, and her legs around his hips, and he pulled himself into her.

You are so beautiful.
You are a miracle.
You are so good.
You are so strong.

* * *

After, they lay side by side, on a cold, smooth rock, the heated vapor coming off the pool and their own supercharged skin keeping them warm.

"So," she said, utterly content, "this is what it feels like to be a sinner."

She wondered, really, why she had waited so long. All through Felix's long illness, people had told her what a saint she was, until she had hated that label.

"If we're sinners," he said, "why do I feel I'm right at heaven's gate?"

The sinner and the saint, she thought, resided side by side in most people, probably in about equal measure, circumstances drawing out one or the other.

It was life in balance, really.

Like this rock they were lying on, hot and cold residing side by side in the perfect unison of healing.

A phrase ran through her head, and she was vaguely aware it was from the story of Adam and Eve.

They were naked and not ashamed.

Since the beginning of time, this was what a man and a woman had been meant to feel together.

The sacredness of connection.

It seemed as if the creation that was at the heart of that story was thrumming with life around them.

The entire universe felt as if it was in harmony right now.

Joy and sorrow danced together, like the motes of her father's ashes caught in sunlight, until they melded together, until she could not tell one from the other, and they became neither joy nor sorrow, but that substance that made up life itself.

Hope.

There was such a sense of *rightness* to the way Faith's arms felt, wrapped around Brad, as he guided the quad back down the mountain.

Realistically, it was not that different than when they had headed up Feeney's Pass, but she was not trying to be proper anymore. She was giving herself fully to their connection, nestled comfortably into the back of him, her cheek resting on the back of his shoulder.

Brad was freezing. He had given Faith his shirt to towel off with as best she could, but now that wetness next to his skin was a terrible thing. His hair was also wet, under the helmet, which intensified the feeling of being cold. He hoped he was blocking the worst of the icy wind from her.

Protecting her.

It felt good to be protecting Faith.

Had he been so protective of her when he was young?

He thought, suddenly, of her words: *It's not as if I can get pregnant.*

He slammed to a halt so abruptly that her chin jabbed into his shoulder. He cut the engine, twisted to look at her.

Her hair was ice-tipped where it poked out from under the helmet.

"You weren't pregnant, were you?"

"What?"

"When you left?"

She shook her head, bemused. "No, Brad. I was taking precautions."

"Did we talk about it?"

"Brad! You're making me feel as if I'm on the witness stand for a cold case." She changed her voice, and it became deep, stern. "And what exactly was Mr. Daniels wearing on June sixteenth, thirty-some years ago?"

Not a condom, apparently.

"Sorry," he muttered. He turned back abruptly, facing forward, feeling guilty.

She was taking precautions.

Where had he been? Had they talked about it, or had his brain just been completely on hold, in that stupor of first love, or more bluntly, first sex, that pushed every single other thing out of the way?

Of course, the *first* aspect of it wouldn't explain why he'd gone on to repeat the very same pattern with Cynthia. She had told him she was protected and he'd happily left that responsibility to her.

He restarted the engine and piloted them down

the hill. It was nearly dusk when they pulled up outside of Wolf's Song.

Faith slid off the quad. He could tell she was cold, despite him blocking the wind.

"You look like you need a hot shower," he said.

She pulled off the helmet and ran her fingers through her crushed hair. The curls sprang back, and she grinned at him in a way that made her seem unchanged from her seventeen-year-old self.

She tilted her head and grinned at him. "Are you joining me?"

CHAPTER FIFTEEN

THE TEMPTATION TO join Faith in the shower was nearly overpowering. But Brad made a decision that he was not going to be the same self-centered, instinct-driven jerk he had been when he was eighteen.

"No," he said, his firmness directed at himself more than at her. "Have your shower. I'll find us something for dinner."

Did she look faintly disappointed as she turned and went into Wolf's Song?

Here was the thing. She hadn't been pregnant, but she could have been. Funny, he had not once considered that possibility.

He recalled himself in those younger days. He'd said he loved Faith. And she had pointed out that, at that age, really, what did they know of love?

He had relished every moment with her, but when she had left, she had not trusted him with the truth that her family was in financial distress. He probably hadn't been worthy of it. Full of himself, enjoying the moment, reveling in the exquisite, all-encompassing sensation of his first really physical relationship.

He remembered going to see Max, all those years ago, asking where she was, pleading for information.

In retrospect, Brad was shocked Faith's father had not punched him in the nose. Because that's what he would have done if some young jock had gone after his baby, which he could now clearly see Cassie had been at seventeen.

But now, Brad thought, as he contemplated how he and Faith had slipped so naturally back into intimacy, he had the rarest of things.

A second chance.

An opportunity to get it so right this time.

Did he love her? Despite the self-centeredness of his eighteen-year-old self, he had been sure he loved her then.

Sure, almost from the first minute he'd seen her, the new girl in town, when she'd arrived at their school at the end of the eleventh grade.

He remembered saying to his mom, getting ready for senior prom, "I'm going to marry Faith Cameron someday."

Since then, though, love had taught him so many hard lessons about loss and powerlessness.

Maybe the new mature him didn't need to think of Faith in terms of love. Instead, he would see that he'd been given an opportunity to have a relationship with his equal, and an adult.

To treat her with respect.

And honor.

To spoil her rotten.

He didn't recall spoiling her rotten having anything to do with their twelfth-grade romance. He recalled almost everything in his young—and, admittedly, exceedingly horny—mind had been being about finding ways to be alone with her.

No wonder she had left without a backward glance.

And yet, he had felt as if he loved her madly, and beyond reason. Still, he was aware, again, he would want to kill anyone who had treated Cassie the way he had treated Faith.

After he had dropped off Faith, he parked the quad at his place. He raced in, and after changing into a dry shirt, and brushing his teeth, and running a comb through helmet-flattened hair, he took out his replacement phone and looked at it for the first time all day.

It occurred to him that it might have been years since he had not looked at his phone for this many hours.

It felt amazing. Freeing.

There were several messages. The first was from the police saying Faith's purse had been turned in.

He contemplated his sense of disappointment. No doubt that meant she would be able to go home Friday, as planned. Today was Tuesday. That would mean only two more full days together.

Somehow, he had hoped to stretch out that *spoiling time*. And maybe he still could. He could just ask her to stay longer, couldn't he?

The other message was from Cassie. Thankfully, she sounded annoyed rather than frightened by his sudden disappearance.

What should he tell her?

Nothing.

The loss of Cynthia had made him and Cassie unusually close, but maybe it was time to back off from that a little.

His daughter did not need to know all the details of his personal life, particularly given the fact she might place herself in charge of a romance project, and she also seemed to think his and Faith's experience out on the ice could be used to benefit the lodge.

He called her.

"What's going on with your phone, Dad?"

He told her about it blowing up over the rescue on the ice so badly he'd had to put it away and temporarily get a new number.

"I've seen pictures of that rescue now. That photographer posted some on social media, with the caption 'do you know these people?' It sure looks like you. The other person looks like a little kid, but I hear it was a woman. The whole town is talking about it."

Yay.

"Another media person posted an interview online with the lady whose dog it was. Its name was Felix. So adorable!"

"That dog was about the furthest thing from adorable that I can think of."

He didn't like it, one little bit, that something that was so highly personal to Faith—her husband's name—was out there in the public. Was it just local, so far? Or was it spreading?

It felt as if the jackals were circling, playing on the fact that everybody would think that was a heartwarming, poignant story. They would only like it *better* if they ever discovered that she had gone after that dog because it shared the same name as her now deceased husband.

But her pain being on display for the world would cause Faith so much suffering. She specifically did not want her daughter to know. He was going to have to look it up himself and see if the story was gaining steam or if it had stalled. He didn't want to ask Cassie because the less he expressed interest in it with her, the better.

"Dad, you should talk to them."

"Them?"

"The media. That photographer was in here again today."

"Did you let him know Gregor's gone?"

"No!"

He wished there was a way to tell Cassie that Faith needed the same kind of protection that his daughter went to such lengths to give their celebrity guests.

But how to make that request without letting on how deeply he was getting involved?

"Because they're going to run with it, anyway, and you probably have the best perspective of the whole thing."

Yes, he did, and knowing the secret of why Faith had gone out on that ice was something he planned to keep to himself.

He didn't like it that they were circling, closer and closer, to Faith's life.

"I'm not talking to them," he said firmly.

"I still think…"

He let her tell him what she thought, but didn't offer any comment. She sighed.

"You're so stubborn sometimes!"

"Now you know where you got it from."

She laughed, forgiving him.

"How was your day?" he asked her, and just as he had hoped, it threw her off the scent of the rescue-on-the-ice story. He listened to her talk about Christmas, how she was going to start on the cottages first—she was thinking of changing out the lights from white to colored around Cobalt Lake, she couldn't find some ornament or other, but she had found the perfect tree…

He was aware, a little ashamed, that he wasn't really listening to her. No, he was ticking off things he needed to get done in his head.

The first thing he did when he hung up was look for the rescue story online. It didn't pop up immediately, which was a good thing. When he found it, the video was pretty lousy. Maybe Gopher needed to improve his skills if he was looking for a break, instead of preying off the talent of others. It had about five thousand views, which in the online world was next to nothing. All it meant was that half the population of Whistler had had a look.

Relieved, he refocused on his mission of making up for the callow young man he had once been.

He snagged another bottle of wine from the very fine collection and then called the Hideaway and placed an order.

Brad hopped in his vehicle and headed into the village. First stop: the cop shop. Though technically the purse probably shouldn't have been surrendered to him, because he was the one who had reported the loss and had standing in the community, and was this week's hero, it was handed over to him without question.

His next stop was the floral shop on Main Street. They were getting ready to close, but again, he was able to use both his community standing and his local-hero status to coax an extraordinary bouquet out of them.

"Something special," he said.

"Any particular color?"

"Maybe just white."

"Budget?"

When was the last time he had purchased flowers? It had been too long, he thought. He wished he would have made small gestures that let his wife know how much he'd appreciated her more common. Marriages would be in a different place if everyone had the awareness he now had, that time was not a guarantee.

"Don't worry about budget," he said, "just the prettiest bouquet you can make."

He exited with a huge paper cone, stunning white blossoms peeking out of it. He wasn't sure what they were, but his whole vehicle filled up with the fragrance.

Then, finally, he stopped at the Hideaway and picked up the dinner he'd ordered for two. By the time he pulled up in front of Wolf's Song, Brad was feeling exceedingly pleased with himself.

Faith opened the door for him, before he even knocked. As if she had been waiting for him.

That did something to his heart.

She had showered and done something with her hair that made all the little curls stand up individually. She'd put on a hint of makeup, which made her eyes look huge and her lips look luscious. She was wearing a white turtleneck sweater, and slacks. It was casual and yet it made her look so feminine and womanly that it would be way too

easy to forget his mission, and behave like a be-
sotted teenage boy all over again.

But what he liked most was when he saw the
light in her face when she took the bouquet from
him and buried her nose in it.

"Did you buy the whole flower shop?" she
teased him.

"I tried," he confessed.

"Gardenias!" she said. "They last about three
seconds, so such a treat! Hydrangeas and roses.
All my favorites!"

He would have liked to have been able to say to
his daughter, *See, Cassie? Panic room? Are you
kidding? The old man doesn't need any help from
you in the romance department.*

"Do you want the good news or the bad news?"
he said, stepping back from the door.

"Okay," she said, "I've fallen for this twice, so
give me the bad news."

He laughed. "There isn't any."

Well, that wasn't exactly true. There was the
video that had popped up online. He reminded
himself to look again later and assess what was
happening with the number of views. He didn't
want her to worry if it was nothing, a local story
that stayed that way.

He held up a finger to her, then went back to
the truck, and came back up the walkway with the
bag of food from the Hideaway. He had tucked
the bottle of wine inside.

Faith took the bag, looked at the restaurant label on it and met his eyes with gratitude.

And then, he turned back once more to his vehicle, and came up the walk with her purse. Her mouth fell open. She nearly dropped the bag of food—with that very expensive wine in it!—but she caught herself, and instead, she set it down, took her purse from him and hugged it.

With those huge eyes so intense and soft on his face, she said, with the faint disbelief of someone who no longer believed good things could happen to her, "It really is all wonderful news."

Brad felt as if it had just become his life mission to keep it that way.

Faith could not believe she was holding her purse! It was such a relief and such a gift. She had just finished a conversation with Maggie, on the borrowed phone, before Brad had arrived.

She had been right about one thing. Maggie had spent much of the day figuring out how to get her home. It involved filing police reports, swearing affidavits, showing up at the airline customer-service hours before the flight. It had felt overwhelming, and like it would take up a great deal of the time she had left here.

And now, she had been granted a reprieve. She could just focus on *this*.

This really being *him*.

She had told Maggie, briefly, about the beautiful releasing of Max's ashes, but nothing else about the day.

Well, what was she going to say?

Oh, by the way, Maggie, you know that guy you thought was so gorgeous? He's actually my first love from high school and we did a very sexy version of mud-wrestling and I can't wait to see what the evening has in store.

Even a sanitized version would have probably given Maggie fits and led to stern advice-giving. It seemed like there was a growing list of things she was keeping from Maggie.

Well, she could let her know one thing that would reduce Maggie's worries. While Brad carried items to the kitchen, she pulled her phone out of the side pocket on her purse. Amazingly, it still had a tiny bit of battery life, and so Faith sent a quick text.

Purse found!

She added a few smiley faces.

"What can I do?" she asked, following Brad into the kitchen.

"You can sit right over there, look beautiful and try this wine."

Faith felt like the princess her father had once wanted her to be, as Brad completely pampered her. He poured wine and set the bottle on the table.

It was even more exquisite than it had been the night before.

"Do you need to charge that phone?" He flipped open a panel behind her that completely concealed a charging station.

Was there anything they hadn't thought of at this resort?

She plugged in her nearly dead phone, and then decided to look up the wine. Maggie would be impressed if she served such an impressive vintage at Christmas dinner.

She stared at her phone, disbelieving. They certainly wouldn't be having it with Christmas dinner.

Now, she wasn't sure what to do. She didn't want to appear gauche, but surely he must have opened this bottle by mistake.

"Brad," she squeaked, "do you know what this wine is worth?"

"No," he said, unconcerned.

"It's worth eight thousand dollars a bottle."

He stopped what he was doing, obviously as startled as she had been. And then he started to laugh. "Oh, well, we can't put the cork back in, so we might as well enjoy it."

"But where did it come from?"

"We have a private cellar, separate from the resort. I'm afraid I have no idea what anything in there is worth. I told you, I'm not much of a wine guy."

She got it. Like the suitcases, the wine must have been his wife's thing.

"I don't think I can enjoy it, now," she said. She used her phone to do some quick calculations. "It's approximately fifty-three dollars and thirty-three cents a sip!"

"All the more reason to enjoy it," he said. He took a small taste out of his glass. "Ah. Fifty-three, thirty-three." And then he took another one. "One hundred and six, sixty-six. One fifty-nine, ninety-nine."

She started laughing. "Please stop."

But he didn't. "Am I impressing you with my math skills?"

"Brad," she said with a sigh of surrender, "you're impressing me in every possible way there is to be impressed."

He grinned at her, pleased, and she found herself relaxing, as he set the table, lit candles, plated the food.

There was an awareness of him, physically, that was startling. The squareness of his wrists, the shape of his fingers, the sensual curve of his lips, his economy of movement as he worked in the kitchen, his innate air of confidence.

He was really so out of her league in every single way! And yet, here she was, Brad Daniels's lover.

CHAPTER SIXTEEN

"BON APPÉTIT," Brad said, setting a plate in front of her with a flourish, and then sliding onto the deeply upholstered bench seat beside her, so close their shoulders were touching.

The scent of him mingled with the scent of food.

The afternoon's escapades—never mind drinking an eight-thousand-dollar bottle of wine—seemed to have left her senses heightened, acutely so. Even though she was wearing a sweater, she could still feel the fabric of his shirt against her shoulder, and beneath that the sinewy strength of him.

She sighed with pleasure, and took a bite of the food.

"This is delicious," Faith said. "I don't even want to know what it cost."

"In comparison to the wine? Peanuts."

"Thank goodness." She took another bite. "I think what we had last night was just as good."

"Take that, Hideaway. I'm going to tell Anita,

our chef who prepared last night's meal. She'll be so pleased. Our restaurant is a little competitive."

Faith liked these small things about him so, so much. He was a man with an eight-thousand-dollar bottle of wine in his cellar and an innovation investor with a portfolio that was probably worth billions, and yet, Brad would take time out of what was no doubt a very busy schedule to make sure one of the staff felt valued.

Unlike his mother, she thought, but brushed the feeling away. Tonight, particularly with her purse back, it felt like she needed to just relax. Enjoy what was being given to her.

He insisted on cleaning up after, and she let him, since really, it just involved scraping the plates and loading the dishwasher.

The fire had not been started, and Faith liked watching Brad's easy competence with it. Paper, kindling, small pieces of wood, match, then a slow feeding of larger pieces until a cheery fire crackled invitingly.

Then he settled on the couch beside her, and threw a companionable arm over her shoulder, kicked off his shoes and put up his feet.

She admired his socks: bright yellow tonight, with orange and black.

He squinted at them. "I think they're ducks," he said, wagging his feet at her. She looked more closely. Definitely ducks!

"You know what duck rhymes with?" he whispered evilly in her ear.

"Truck," she ventured, pretending innocence.

"Exactly!"

After a moment, he leaned over and said, his tone husky and suggestive, "Do what you're dying to do."

What she was dying to do was so X-rated it made her blush.

"I mean we're halfway down that road, anyway," he whispered. "With ducks and trucks."

She held her breath, thinking of the word she *never* said, that rhymed with both of those.

"Go ahead," Brad said softly, pulling away from her just enough to let his gaze slide to her lips.

She leaned toward him, her eyes half-closed.

"We both know what you're dying to do. That's a fast charger. Your phone is probably ready to go. So show me the pictures of your grandchildren."

Faith burst out laughing. She loved it that he was teasing her. She loved how easily the laughter came. She gave Brad a solid thump on his shoulder. "That's not what I thought you were going to say."

"Really?" He lifted a sexy eyebrow. "Dirty mind."

"Maybe we should give the phone a little longer to charge," she suggested.

Without another word, he lifted her against his chest, and she curled her arms around his neck, and snuggled into him. He carried her down the hall and into that bedroom as if she was light as a feather.

He put her down on the bed, and they undressed each other, with wonder and deliberation. This wasn't something that was *just happening*, as it had been at the Mud Puddle. This was a choice.

They used every inch of that bed, which just yesterday, she had thought was so ridiculously large.

This second time, there was an exquisitely slow tenderness to their lovemaking. They were two people who had been cast adrift, who had found each other. Who were rescuing each other, who were celebrating being pulled back from the abyss of a dark, roiling, endless, uncertain sea.

Much later, Brad, completely naked, completely confident in his nakedness, padded out of the room to retrieve her phone. Oh, those dimples!

Faith was pretty amazed by how she didn't feel self-conscious, either. Was there an opposite to self-consciousness?

If there was, he had drawn it out of her. With his hands and his lips and the look in his eyes.

It might be, she mused, with him out of the room, a good time to ask herself where all this was going. But the truth was, she didn't care.

She had cared all her life. She had made plans, lived by rules and behaved a certain way, and despite her best efforts, nothing had turned out the way she expected it to, anyway.

Now, for once, she would try to just breathe. To just enjoy, to the fullest, the pure sensual sensation of being in the moment.

He came back in, gave her her phone. Clothed only in sheets, she opened it and showed him some pictures.

"This is Maggie and Michael," she said. It was a picture taken of them in front of the Christmas tree, last year.

"They're extraordinarily beautiful," Brad said. "Maggie looks a lot like your dad. Your son has your hair. Look at that mop of curls. I bet he has to fight the girls off."

When she looked at this picture, though, she didn't see how gorgeous Michael was. She saw the tension around his mouth, the baffled anger. Would she ever be able to overcome the barriers he had erected around himself, as if family was so painful for him, he no longer wanted to be a part of one?

"Everything okay?" Brad asked, pushing a little strand of hair away from her forehead with his thumb.

He was so sensitive to her.

"Felix being so changed was really hard on the kids. I can see it in Michael's face in this picture."

"You are undoubtedly an extraordinary mom.

I'm going to say you gave them what they needed to come back from it."

How had he happened on the most perfect thing to say?

"These are my grandchildren, Tanya and Chloe."

"There's those curls again," he said, as if those curls were the most amazing thing in the entire world!

The image was of them in the kitchen, the girls on chairs, in aprons she had made them for Christmas, wooden spoons raised to lips, a big green bowl between them.

"That's the cookie bowl," she said, and then glanced at him. In his glamorous world, did it all seem just a little domestic and dull?

But if the smile tickling across his lips was any indication, no.

"Your face," he said, handing her back the phone, and touching her cheek with a fingertip, "when you look at those girls."

"You'll know someday."

He sighed. "I hope."

"Show me your daughter."

"I'm still on the temp phone."

"Oh, no. Is your phone still blowing up?"

He shrugged. "I haven't looked at it all day. Such a sense of reprieve. I'll grab the temporary one, though, and see if I can pull up her social-media page."

So Faith and Brad sat in that huge bed—it could

have been a twin for as much of it as they were using—backs propped up on luscious pillows, swathed in crisp white Egyptian cotton sheets, admiring each other's families.

When she yawned, he turned off the phone. "Sorry. I forgot the time difference. I'll head out."

"Please stay," she whispered.

He sighed. "I was hoping you'd ask."

And he settled back in the bed beside her, gathered her in her arms and took her all the way home.

Just before she slept, she thought of how just last night this bed had seemed too big and too lonely. In her journey through grief, this is what she had least expected.

How swift and bright was the light of hope. With those thoughts swirling around her, Faith thought she would have the best sleep ever.

Instead, she woke to pitch-blackness, trembling from the remnants of a terrible dream.

"Hey," Brad said softly, and Faith found his arms around her. "I think you had a bad dream. You were yelling."

He pulled her close to him, nuzzled her neck, buried his nose in her hair.

"I did have a bad dream," she said, shaken, so comforted by his arms and his warmth in the bed.

"Tell me," he invited huskily, and nudged her to turn over and face him. Her eyes were adjusting to the dark, and she took in the lines of his face, the sweep of his lashes, the curve of his lips.

She felt safe, the opposite of how the dream had made her feel.

"Tell me," he said again.

And so she did.

"I was out walking in a park in Toronto," she said, taking strength from the beautiful calm of his dark eyes. "It was a nice summer day, and there were lots of people in the park. Families picnicking, young couples strolling hand in hand, little kids laughing. And then this loose dog came toward me. He was quite lovely, a big dog with a thick brown fur coat, and soft eyes. It was really friendly, wagging its tail, its tongue hanging out, almost like it was grinning.

"I stood still and the dog came to me, and I was so delighted, like somehow it had picked me out of all the people in the park that day.

"But when I reached down to pet it—more like to welcome it—it turned into a bear. And it stood up on its hind legs and it grabbed me in this hold. It was so strong. It was crushing me. I couldn't get away. That's probably when you heard me yelling because then I woke up."

"That's powerful," he said. "I see a pretty clear meaning in it."

"I agree. I have variations of it, all the time. This is the first time with the dog, though. It's a dream where I think I'm safe and happy, and I'm amazed I'm the one having this experience.

"But then there's some danger lurking, or something familiar becomes extraordinarily terrifying without warning. Once I dreamt I was in my kitchen, making cookies, and a gunman burst in, and started shooting everything, my beautiful kitchen being ripped apart by machine-gun blasts."

His arms tightened around her. His silence encouraged her to continue.

"I guess my subconscious is trying to help me deal with my life. Everything that I thought was safe, this feeling of being blessed by love, suddenly being wrecked, turning into something dangerous and unpredictable."

"Faith," he whispered. "I'm so sorry. Did your husband…? Was he dangerous and unpredictable?"

"That was the hardest part. That this kind and dignified and gentle man became a complete stranger to me. It happened slowly. At first, he'd say or do something strange, and I'd just brush it off. 'He's tired. He's stressed. He hasn't been eating right.' My dad hadn't seen him for two years when he came back to Toronto, sick. And he noticed right away that Felix had changed a great deal.

"And then I wasn't so quick to dismiss things. It was quite alarming, watching how reckless he had become, agitated, like a hyperactive child. Forward motion with no thought. So there were accidents, like catching a frying pan on fire, and incidents like getting caught shoplifting in a neighborhood store. He became so unbelievably nasty. He had no filters, whatever he was thinking he just said. He had no comprehension that he was hurting people. Last Christmas, he challenged our son-in-law to a fight. So, yes, I guess he did become dangerous and unpredictable.

"It was even worse because I felt as if I couldn't tell anyone what was going on, because I wanted to protect him. I didn't want people looking at him through the lens of something I had said about him."

"How lonely was that for you?"

"You have no idea."

But his hand squeezing hers made her think maybe he did have an idea.

"The only people I wanted to tell were doctors. I had this naive idea the medical system would step in and help you if things went sideways.

"But that's not how it works, at least not with brain disorders. A doctor, who would spend ten minutes with Felix, would think he knew way more about him than I did after thirty years together. My calls for help—increasingly desperate pleas—felt as if they fell into an abyss. It was so unbelievably hard to get a diagnosis. Because I couldn't get a diagnosis, the kids just thought

Felix was becoming horrible with age, and that I was making excuses for him.

"But in the end, what difference did that diagnosis that I finally got make? There was not a single thing they could do to change it or stop it."

Faith couldn't believe she'd unloaded all of that. She was not sure she had ever told her story so completely.

"You have lived through the nightmare you just woke up from."

"You know what the worst of it was? All these nasty things he was saying and doing? What if the kids were right? What if that's who he always had really been—what if he'd always nursed these horrible thoughts about people—and the disappearance of his filters just allowed it all to come out?"

After a long time, his voice strong, sure, something a person could really hold on to in the dark of night, Brad said, "I don't believe that."

"Why not?"

"First of all, you would have never married a man like that. But second, you know how people are when they're drunk? You know how they say and do all kinds of things they would never normally say and do?"

She could not help but think of her father at her wedding.

"There's a saying—*in vino veritas*. It's Latin, it means 'in wine there is truth,' but I've never quite seen it that way, either. Cassie had a friend once, in her teen years, the sweetest girl you could ever meet. Kind, helpful, quiet. Cassie brought her home one night after they'd had too much to drink. She was so awful. Loud, rude, vulgar. The next day she didn't even remember. But how could anyone look at her and reach the conclusion that how she behaved, for those few hours out of her whole life, was who she was?

"It's an altered state. It's not who people really are," Brad concluded quietly. "And I'm sure that's what it was for Felix, too."

She felt an amazing wash of peace when he said that. A sense of understanding, not just for Felix, but for her father, too.

"Thank you," she whispered to him. "Those are just about the most comforting words anyone has ever said to me about this."

CHAPTER SEVENTEEN

FAITH FELL ASLEEP AGAIN, but Brad didn't. He marveled at the way he felt with her in his arms.

The truth was, he hadn't ever thought he would feel this way again.

Whole.

Complete.

So, so alive.

It was very much like that eighteen-year-old boy who had declared with such fierce certainty, *I'm going to marry Faith Cameron someday.*

He felt wildly and ridiculously in love, as if his every sense was humming, vibrating electrically within him.

He couldn't just come out and say that. A declaration of love at this early stage would scare Faith into next week. After all, he was even scaring himself.

But he could *show* her. Slowly, he could try and heal what the last few years had given her. He could do that by giving her these last two days and making them as carefree, as fun and as full of adventure as was possible.

Wednesday and Thursday. Friday she was supposed to go home.

But maybe, if the next two days went well, he could convince her to stay.

He could see if what he thought he was feeling could stand up to the kind of reality tests only time could give it.

He couldn't change what had happened to her, or the way his teenage self had behaved, but he could make her laugh.

Feel young again.

Have hope.

Embrace adventure.

Feel confident in her own beauty.

Maybe even have faith, as her name called her to do. That life would be good again. That the dogs would not turn into bears, that she could feel safe and secure even if she was doing things that weren't exactly safe and secure.

"What are we doing here?" she asked, the next morning, getting out of his car. Brad had been up since 5:00 a.m. laying the groundwork for this. "What is this place?"

"It's a zip line."

She digested that for about two seconds. "What a terrible idea."

But underneath the words, he heard the fear of a woman who had friendly dogs turn into killer bears in her dreams. And in her real life.

"It's not such a bad idea," he said softly. "An adventure like this is about facing your fears. It's about discovering your competence in dealing with them. Life throws us all kinds of stuff. We can't control that. The one thing we can control is ourselves."

This is part of what he had learned in search-and-rescue.

"The way I see it, life has thrown some unbelievable stuff at you. Stuff you probably thought would crush you. But it hasn't. Embrace that. This lesson is as much for me as it is for you. Do you know I haven't skied since Cynthia died?"

As he knew it would, as soon as he made it about a benefit to him—about helping him—she was right on board.

She took a deep breath, and regarded the course, and then they walked up to the entrance kiosk. It was such an act of trust.

She laughed when she saw the sign on the window, not even trying to hide her relief. "Look, it's closed for the day. A private event."

He laughed, too. "The private event is us."

"What?"

"It's not their busy time of year. I didn't want to have to worry about either of us being recognized."

She actually put her hands on her hips and glared at him. He thought he'd better not smile, even though she looked as adorable as an angry kitten.

"You booked the whole park?"

"I did."

"Don't you think that's unnecessarily extravagant?" she asked him sternly.

"Hey, it doesn't even hold a candle to that wine last night."

"I think your money would be better used for something else."

He was not entirely certain she wasn't just using this indignation as a shield to avoid zip-lining.

"Such as?" he challenged her.

"How about the food bank?" she ventured.

He gave her a long look, then pulled his phone—still the temporary one—out of his pocket. He couldn't remember the accountant's phone number, but he found the website and dialed it that way.

He got by reception with ease.

"Graham. How are you? Brad Daniels here… Cassandra's fine, she's getting the place ready for Christmas. How about Brenda?" After they got the pleasantries dealt with—Graham's daughter, who had gone to school with Cassie, was expecting grandchild number three—he said, "Speaking of Christmas, I'd like to make a donation to the hamper fund at the food bank… Oh. I already have? How much?… Okay. Double that."

He clicked off his phone and put it in his pocket.

"Now, you're just showing off," she said, but a smile was tickling her lips.

"Just trying to impress my lady. Did it work?"

"Oh, yeah," she said softly. She took a deep breath. Her grip tightened on his. "Okay," she said, "I'll do this."

"It's just the beginning," he said. "I have a few other things planned, too."

She regarded him thoughtfully for a minute. Then she said, "Okay, Brad, you can have the rest of today. But tomorrow, I'm going to make the plans."

He frowned at that. He had it all in place for tomorrow night. He looked at his watch. Maybe, he could move it up to tonight.

"If you'll excuse me just a sec, I have to make another phone call."

A few minutes later, he stood on the precipice, harnessed in and wearing a helmet. He helped Faith buckle hers in place.

"If this is so safe, why are we wearing helmets?" she demanded. "And what possible good will they do as we are falling to our deaths?"

"We won't die of a head injury?" he teased her. "You first, my lady."

"No, no, you first. I insist."

"Okay, but you have to promise you won't chicken out and leave me stranded on the next platform by myself."

"Okay," she said. "I promise."

Her promise felt as if it carried the weight of a cargo full of gold.

Brad was surprised his hands were a bit clammy. He couldn't let Faith see that. He'd never get her to go. He took a deep breath, and pushed off the first platform. The harness caught him, and suddenly he was whooshing through the air at breakneck speed.

He realized the sensation of a total loss of control was not one he particularly liked. He had to clamp his jaws shut to keep from yelling his dismay. He was very happy when his feet found the next platform.

He turned and gave Faith a thumbs-up, hoping she wouldn't be able to see the slight shaking in his hands. She squinted at him, took a deep breath and leaped.

What had he done? She was screaming in terror! But then he realized, it wasn't terror at all! She was screaming with laughter.

Her feet found the platform and she tumbled into his arms, gazing up at him with absolute delight.

"That was the best! The wind! The feeling of freedom! It was like flying." She suddenly stopped, and looked at him more closely.

"You didn't like it," she said, despite his best effort at a brave expression.

"Terrified," he admitted, pressing his forehead to hers. Just like that, she was the strong one. He saw exactly how she had gotten through Felix's illness. Because she had a core of pure steel.

She leaned into him, and whispered, "Brad, it's the closest sensation to sex I've ever had without actually having sex."

"That puts an entirely different spin on it," he said.

"I hoped it would."

And somehow, after that, he surrendered to it. To the speed, and the sense of not being in control, and of the bottom falling out of his belly and his world. He loved how she imparted her joy and her confidence into him.

He realized that discovering something brand-new, even if it was frightening, gave the world a shimmer it had not had before. Or maybe that shimmer was from sharing the brand-new experience with her, just as they had when they were younger.

A few hours later, Faith stood in front of him. He helped her unsnap her harness. The look on her face made the private booking of the zip line a bargain. It would have been a bargain at twice the price.

"I *loved* that," she said, unnecessarily, since her enjoyment was shining out of her eyes.

"Me, too," he agreed, and realized he really, really meant it.

"I think that's the most exhilarating thing I've ever done," she told him.

"Since you've already compared it to sex, my ego feels quite deflated," he said, for her ears only, with mock sullenness.

"Okay, the most exhilarating family-friendly thing I've ever done. I'm going to see if there's any zip lines close to us in Toronto. I mean, the girls are too young, but it would be a great thing for Maggie and Michael and Sean and I to do together. It's exactly as you promised, a chance to embrace the exhilarating side of fear."

He liked it *so* much that her first thought was how to share an experience like this with the people who meant the most to her.

"I have something even better planned for tonight," he told her.

"Better than that?" she said skeptically.

"I think so. It's formal, though."

"I didn't bring anything formal to wear."

"Go get something. You never had a chance to use that preloaded credit card I gave you." He sighed at the look on her face. "I'll make another donation to the food bank."

At this rate, the recipients of his generosity would be having steak and lobster for Christmas dinner rather than turkey.

"How formal?" she asked him a little later as he dropped her off in front of Wolf's Song.

"As formal as you can make it." He looked at his watch. "I'll pick you up at six."

Faith entered a Whistler boutique that she would have never ever been able to afford when she lived here. She remembered how stressed she had been going to prom.

She had taken the sea-to-sky shuttle into Vancouver and used her chambermaid earnings to buy an exquisite dress at a secondhand store. She had traveled that distance so that none of her classmates would see her dress and recognize it as one they had discarded.

She had owned many gorgeous gowns since then, for faculty events, weddings, graduations, alumni reunions. And she had never owned another secondhand one. But she had never owned one like this shop was selling, either.

In fact, this was the kind of shop she avoided. The tasteful displays, soft lighting, good furniture, mirrors with gilt around the edges might as well have been neon signs blinking *expensive*. She had always harbored a secret sense that the sales staff in a place like this would know an impostor when they saw one!

But it must have been a new staff member today, because she didn't have the good sense to kick Faith out as not belonging.

In fact, she smiled at her, waved a hand and called, "Let me know if I can help you find something."

Which was probably the same as saying "I won't bother, because I can tell you can't afford it."

She went to a rack of evening dresses, and flipped over a price tag on a midnight-blue one.

She tried not to gasp. On the other hand, the man had probably spent the equivalent of a new car on her today.

She could suck it up for once in her life.

The saleslady materialized at her side, as if she knew, somehow, a decision had been made. But she wasn't in the least snooty. In fact, she reminded Faith of one of Maggie's friends who went to the young-mothers group.

"I'm Bridgette," she introduced herself.

"A special-occasion dress?" she clarified once Faith had told her what she was looking for. "My favorite. I've got just the one. I thought of it the minute I saw you looking at this rack. Come with me."

And just like that, Faith found herself in a very posh changing room, looking at herself in the most gorgeous gown she had ever laid eyes on.

A little later, handing over her own credit card, not the one Brad had given her, she was not sure that how wonderful she felt buying that dress could be considered sucking it up.

That parcel tucked under her arm, Faith's next stop was the grocery store. She felt, acutely, the juxtaposition of the dress with her purchases there.

Perhaps she could change her plan for tomorrow. But really, there wasn't time. And in a way, it was a bit of a test.

Hours later, despite wearing a dress about equal to a month's salary when she'd been teaching,

Faith felt as nervous waiting for Brad to come as she had felt all those years ago in her secondhand dress for prom.

She looked at herself in the mirror.

The dress was dazzling and elegant. Like Brad's hair, all the shades of gray in the silky fabric reminded her of storm clouds with the light behind them. The dress was beautifully cut, with a deep V at both the front and back, belted at the waist and then flaring out to midcalf. This was obviously why people paid so much for these dresses: the design of it *loved* how women were made. It hugged all the best parts of her and skimmed over others.

She looked beautiful.

And yet, when she looked at herself, she was aware the beauty did not come from the dress, or from her painstakingly tamed hair and her carefully applied makeup.

The beauty was from surviving the lake.

The beauty was from riding behind Brad on the quad.

The beauty was from honoring her father's last wish.

The beauty was from allowing herself to experience every single pleasure the Mud Puddle had offered her.

And the beauty was from having loved—and lost—and somehow finding within herself the courage to try it all again.

The doorbell rang, and, feeling really nervous for some reason, Faith opened the door.

Brad stood there looking very James Bondish, in a black jacket, a crisp pleated shirt, a bow tie, knife-pressed black slacks and mirror-polished black dress shoes. Gregor Watson did not have a single thing on him.

She was glad for every cent she had spent on that dress, but she wasn't sure even that was enough to bolster her confidence in light of how suavely perfect he was.

"Show me the socks," she whispered.

He lifted a pant leg, and he had on blue socks with purple polka dots. Just like that, he was *her* Brad again, fun-loving, devoted to his daughter, not taking himself too seriously. She didn't need to be the least self-conscious of him.

Tonight, he had a different vehicle, parked in front of Wolf's Song, sporty and low-slung, and nearly as hard to get into as his bigger SUV had been.

Of course, the shoes were unreasonable. But she'd had to have them. And her new best friend Bridgette had insisted.

They weren't in the car very long. In fact, he drove around the corner, to the bottom of the Timber Wolf run and the chairlift station.

She gave him a quizzical look, but he stopped the car, came around and opened her door. He guided her through the dark to the front of the station.

A voice greeted them. "Evening, Mr. Daniels. Ma'am."

Brad took her hand and settled her on the waiting chair. The lift attendant handed him a thick blanket and Brad put it over her shoulders and his, cocooning them together.

"Thanks, Mel," he said. "Remember—"

"Top secret," the young man said.

Faith shivered with delight. It really was all very secret agent. She loved it. The chairlift hummed to life, clanked once or twice, and then they were riding higher and higher, as the cables lifted them above the ground.

CHAPTER EIGHTEEN

FAITH SNUGGLED INTO Brad and took in the views. Soon, they could see all the way to Whistler. Cobalt Lake and Whistler both looked like miniature Christmas villages, their lights winking in the darkness.

By the time they reached the top station, they were in snow. The moon had risen and the world felt silver and white, as if it had all been designed to match her dress.

It was utterly magical. Adding to the magic, it somehow felt as if taking her to the top of a mountain on a chairlift was a subtle, but beautiful nod, to her father.

The chair halted, and Brad took the blanket from his shoulders and completely wrapped it around her. Even so, it was very cold up here. A path had been shoveled to a small café that Faith recalled served hot chocolate and coffee during the ski season.

Tonight, Brad held open the door for her, and a wall of welcoming warmth embraced her. There was a single, candlelit, white-linen-covered table, set for two, the chairs next to each other, rather than opposite each other, so that they could both face the view.

A formally attired waiter glided out, and filled their wineglasses.

"Don't even ask," Brad warned her.

So she didn't. She didn't ask what the wine had cost, or allow herself to wonder what this exquisite dinner experience had cost him.

The waiter came out again, this time with a tray covered in a silver dome. He set it carefully in the center of the table, and with a flourish removed the cover.

Tears sparked in Faith's eyes. "Oh, Brad," she whispered, as she looked at the two Zippy burgers wrapped in their distinctive red-and-white paper.

"The funny thing is Zippy's is still there, and the place we were supposed to go that night has long since shut down."

It flooded back to her. Prom night. She had felt like Cinderella in the beautiful gown she had managed to pick up secondhand. But she felt like Cinderella in more ways than that. Because Brad had insisted he was picking her up at her place, the run-down trailer on the edge of town.

When she had come out of her room in the gown, Max had stared at her, flummoxed. And then he had bowed before her, and kissed her hand, and asked her for a dance.

Dancing with her dad, she had looked up at him to see the tears in his eyes.

"My little girl," he'd whispered, "all grown up and I'm not ready for it."

And it felt as if it was only then that she, too, had realized exactly what that night represented. A transition. The end of one chapter and the opening of another. High school would be over in a few days.

And then, Brad had arrived, standing nervously at the door with a corsage in his hand, and a limo idling behind him.

Max had put him at ease, chatting and teasing, and then he'd noticed the limo. "Wow," he said to Faith, "you're beating your old man to a first ride in a limousine."

And then Brad, with that amazing generosity of spirit that had made her love him, had said, "We're going for dinner first, Mr. Cameron, why don't you come with us?"

Faith supposed there were some girls who wouldn't have liked that. But somehow, to her, it felt perfect, saying goodbye to this part of her life with the two men she loved most.

And so the three of them had climbed into the limo, her and Max equally as wide-eyed and how luxurious it was. And then Max had said, "My treat tonight, kids." And he'd tapped on the glass and said, "Zippy's and step on it."

And so instead of the dinner at the fancy restaurant where Brad had reservations, the limo had pulled up in front of Zippy's and let them out. It shone in her memory. Maybe because it was so soon after that everything fell apart.

"Funny," she said, "how sometimes when things don't go according to plan, they turn out so perfectly."

"One of the best nights ever," Brad told her quietly, and raised his wineglass to her. "To remembering old memories and making new ones."

After the dinner things had been cleared away, the transformed café was filled with music and Brad held out his hand to her.

They danced together.

Again, she was drawn back to senior prom, to how it had felt to sway against him, how aware she had been of every detail of him: his scent, the thickness of his lashes, the full bottom lip, the way his hand had felt resting on her waist.

She gazed up at him now and felt that familiar intensity.

"You know what I love best about an older Faith?" he asked softly.

"What?"

"Everything," he responded with such sincerity her heart stopped.

"Oh, Brad," she said, "wrinkles and extra pounds—"

He put a finger to her lips. "Life," he said. "When I look at you, I see your life in your eyes. I see the layers of it. I see you holding sick kids in the middle of the night, and choosing a prom dress with your own daughter. I see you and Felix making sacrifices so that she can become a lawyer and Michael can go to Scotland. I see the depth facing sorrow has given you. And I see the courage in your undiminished capacity for joy."

Out the expanse of windows, the stars twinkled above them, and the lights of the village twinkled below.

Faith was so deliciously aware that somehow she had left her real life behind her and stepped directly into a fairy tale.

Only Brad was saying this was the *real* her.

Just as it was the real him. He had grown into his great promise of generosity, of humor, of sensitivity.

She melted further into him, felt the cradle of his arms close around her, and wished for this to never, ever end.

It was the wee hours of the morning before they were back at Wolf's Song. They fell into each other's arms.

Despite the exhaustion, a need was there, that had been building and building as they had danced together on the top of that mountain. It was as quiet as the hum of a bee, as immutable as the waves of the ocean, as powerful as a sudden summer storm.

They undressed each other with reverence, they worshipped at the altar of life. Faith had a sense of each of them bringing everything they had ever been, everything they now were and everything they would ever be.

They began as separate people, kissing, tasting, touching, giving and receiving pleasure, exploring sensuality from a lovely place of maturity. But as the intensity built between them, the sense of separateness was lost.

Not just between them. As they exploded, the barriers of the universe came down, and they collapsed. Into everything.

She lay in the circle of Brad's arms after, feeling the steady rise and fall of his naked chest beneath her cheek.

Beyond content.

Happy.

She was the one thing she had wondered if she could ever be again. She marveled at it. She was happy.

The smallest niggling of doubt pierced that happiness. She'd volunteered to make the plan for tomorrow.

What could she give the man who had everything?

Especially since his daughter had already beaten her to the sock idea?

She could give him the one thing he had missed.

But suddenly, in the light of everything he had given her, her humble, homey idea felt *not good enough*.

Tomorrow felt as if it was going to be a test. She fit into his world. Would he fit into hers? Somehow, she didn't feel ready for that test, or for the possible answer.

But it was too late to make a different plan.

In the morning, she was familiarizing herself with the kitchen when he came in. He was so darned cute first thing with his tousled hair, and sleepy, sexy eyes.

"I'm going to go to my place and grab a shower and a change of clothes. Any wardrobe suggestions for your plan?"

Insecurity clawed at her. No fancy dress required. No quad helmets. No adventure-sturdy mountain wear.

She was going to introduce Brad to ordinary life. After the magical worlds he had invited her into, it was sure to fall flat.

Faith debated canceling.

She debated telling him he could come up with the plan for the day, after all.

But no, it was time to see if their worlds had any overlap at all.

"No," she said, "just come dressed for comfort."

He came and kissed her, full on the lips, and it almost made her insecurities vanish. Almost.

"So what's the plan?" he said, when he arrived back.

Comfy for him was a pair of dark denim jeans,

a crisp shirt paired with them. He looked way too sexy for what she had in mind.

She took a deep breath. "We're going to bake cookies this morning."

She watched him closely for signs: that it was too domestic for him, a little dull, boring.

Instead, he grinned at her with such real enthusiasm that she felt her heart melt. In fact, it felt as if any little piece of herself she had been holding back from him, suddenly and completely surrendered.

"Look what I found," she said, leading him over to the counter.

He looked at her find. "I don't have a clue what that is. A device dropped from the ship of an extraterrestrial?"

He was going to make the differences in their worlds seem fun, like exploring a new place.

"It's a stand mixer!"

He inspected it. "As opposed to a sitting mixer?"

"It's a chef-worthy piece of equipment. What kind of vacation cottage is equipped like this?"

"This cottage actually has a commercial kitchen, because it's the largest of the cottages. Sometimes people rent all of the cottages, particularly in the offseason, for weddings or conferences or family reunions. This one becomes the central meeting place, and it's set up for caterers."

Soon, they were measuring ingredients together.

He had put on his playlist. The kitchen was filled with sunshine, laughter and music.

She handed him one of the beaters after they had creamed all the cookie ingredients together. She took the other one for herself. She licked the cookie dough off it.

"Oh, my," he said, watching her with narrowed eyes. "So that's how you learned to do all those remarkable things with your tongue."

He closed his eyes, and began to do very wickedly exaggerated things to the beater with his tongue and lips. Soon, he was adding sounds, until he had her howling with laughter.

In fact, she had never laughed so much while baking cookies in her entire life.

Now, the first batch of cookies was cooling on the counter, and the second was in the oven. He was sitting, casually, on the island. She had taken the beaters out of the beautiful stand mixer that was built into the cabinet system.

It occurred to Faith she had wanted to show Brad what ordinary looked and felt like. Instead, he had shown her the extraordinary hidden among the ordinary.

Suddenly, without anyone knocking or the bell ringing, the front door swung open. Brad slid off the counter and turned to it, quizzically.

Faith recognized his daughter. Cassie came in and pecked him on the cheek, took in the cookies, acknowledged Faith with a lifted hand.

Faith noticed Brad had set the beater down, almost as if he was hiding it. In fact, he had a bit of a deer-caught-in-the-headlights look.

"I thought I'd start Christmas decorations over here later this afternoon. I don't like to do the public areas until after Remembrance Day, but I thought I could get a head start on this."

"Sure," Brad said. Faith tilted her head at him. It was their last full day together, and her plan for the afternoon hadn't involved working around his daughter setting up Christmas decorations.

"Dad, you must be in charge of cookies for the next search-and-rescue meeting. I think hiring a caterer is cheating."

Faith waited for Brad to correct his daughter, and make an introduction.

Instead, Brad said nothing.

His daughter came over and offered her hand. "Hi, I'm Cassandra, Mr. Daniels's daughter."

"Hi, Cassie," Faith said warmly. "I'm Faith." She glanced at Brad. Nothing.

"It's Cassandra," she said. The correction was ever so casual, but it put up the faintest of barriers. The *staff* did not call her Cassie. She helped herself to a cookie, as if she owned the place, which come to think of, she did.

"These are delicious," she said. "Can you make sure Anita gets the recipe?"

"Of course," she said, and heard a bit of tightness in her own voice.

"What time do you think you'll be wrapping up? I won't come in until after you're gone."

Again, here was an opportunity for Brad to indicate Faith was not the caterer, that they were friends. And that the cottage was in use until tomorrow.

When he didn't say anything, Faith said, a little sharply, "Not to worry. I'm done."

Cassandra left with that same surge of busy energy she had come in with.

Faith took off her apron, folded it carefully and set it on the island. "I'm not sure I understand what just happened there, Brad. I thought I was staying here until tomorrow."

She'd also had some pretty hot plans for him this afternoon, that involved that huge, jetted tub in the en suite bathroom, and a container full of rose petals.

"We have lots of rooms," he said with a shrug.

"Why didn't you tell her I wasn't a caterer?" Faith asked softly.

"It just seemed less complicated not to mention it."

Suddenly, it occurred to Faith that the lift attendant last night had been sworn to secrecy, not because of the media chasing a story, but because Brad hadn't wanted his daughter to know about her.

"Really? It never occurred to you that your daughter mistaking me for staff might be hurtful to me, particularly since you didn't seem eager to correct her perception?"

He looked puzzled, the same as when she had mentioned her suitcase not being up-to-snuff.

"I was staff here, once. Do you remember that?"

"You were a chalet girl," he said, eying her uncomfortably, apparently sensing her rising temper and bracing for it.

"A chalet girl. Your mom's euphemism for a chambermaid. You know what I did, Brad? I stripped dirty sheets off beds, and cleaned toilets. I bet you've never done either, have you?"

"I'm not sure where this is going," he said uncomfortably.

"Your mom told me all those years ago that I wasn't good enough for you and I can see nothing has changed. You didn't even introduce me to your daughter!"

"My mom said that to you?" He looked genuinely shocked.

But she had started now, and she couldn't have stopped, even if she wanted to. It felt as if she had been keeping the secret to protect him. But now, she saw she'd been protecting herself, as well, as if the grown-up her might be able to slip into his world, her lack of social standing no longer applicable.

She was telling him *everything*.

"Brad, my dad lost all the money he'd saved for college gambling on a horse. A sure thing, he

said. I'm not sure your mother set that up, though
I wouldn't put it past her. But she sure didn't let
an opportunity get by her to get rid of the *chalet*
girl who had *designs* on her son."

"What are you talking about?" He looked angry
now.

"You know who my mysterious benefactor was?
You know who paid for my college, in the east,
far away from her precious son? You know who
made a stipulation that I wasn't to contact you *at
all*? *Ever?*"

Brad looked utterly stunned.

She marched by him. He reached out to stop
her, but she ducked easily out of his grasp and
kept going.

She went down the hallway, and into the bedroom. She closed the door and locked it behind
her. She ignored his soft knock on the door.

She pulled her shabby suitcase out of the cup-
board, threw things in it, including that stupid bag
full of rose petals she'd saved from the bouquet
he'd bought her. She zipped it shut.

She ignored his rattle of the handle.

"Faith, we need to talk about this."

She pulled out her phone and called the hotel
she'd originally had a reservation with. Thankfully, they had a room available for tonight.

The dress she had worn last night was still
hanging in the closet. She realized she didn't want

it. It was part of a world she could never belong to. One in which she had been an impostor.

She fished through her purse and put the unused credit card he had given her on the dresser.

Taking one last look around, feeling like Cinderella after the clock had struck twelve, Faith opened the double doors that went out to a deck off the bedroom.

She softly closed them and, tugging her suitcase behind her, took the boardwalk around Cobalt Lake toward Whistler.

When she got home, she'd send him a check for the jacket, and the toque and the clothes.

And then she'd burn them.

As she walked around the lake, she could almost see herself, out there, nearly drowning, thinking, laughably, that her father or Felix had somehow taken pity on all her suffering over the past years.

That her fate had been altered.

But she should be way more familiar with fate than that by now.

CHAPTER NINETEEN

I$_{T}$ WAS QUITE a while before Brad realized Faith had left.

He'd gone and sat in the living room, waiting for her to cool off. She would understand when he explained to her that he didn't want Cassie figuring out who she was because of the media thing.

And he certainly didn't want his daughter thinking Faith was a romantic interest.

She'd probably laugh when he told her Cassie would have them locked together in a panic room in no time.

Though if he was going to be locked in a panic room…

A horrible shrill noise startled him and he leaped off the couch. Smoke was roiling out the oven door and the fire alarm was shrieking its outrage.

He went and opened the oven door, and was nearly overcome with smoke inhalation. Brad slammed the door shut, held his breath and then opened it again. He pulled the second batch of now scorched cookies out with a tea towel. In his haste, he burned his hand.

Standing there, sucking on the burn, he waited for the bedroom door to fly open, for Faith to dash out, worried about him. She was the kind who would worry and fuss over any injury. She'd probably want to look at his hand, run it under cold water, insist on a first-aid kit—it might be just the thing to soften that unfamiliar anger he had seen flare up in her eyes.

But the door didn't open.

And then he knew.

She was gone.

The cookies suddenly felt like an illustration of his life: scorched.

He wandered back into the great room, nursing his hand, and sank back down on the couch. Eventually the smoke alarm stopped shrieking. Brad thought about what Faith had accused his mother of.

He wanted, desperately, for it not to be true. But in his heart, he knew it was. The pieces of the puzzle of Faith's sudden departure from his life just fit together a little too snugly.

His world felt strangely perilous, as he challenged what he had believed to be true his entire life. His mother had been part of that life—one of the biggest parts—for forty years. Of course, he'd known she had flaws. His mother had never been going to win a popularity contest. But he would have never imagined she was capable of something so controlling and so conniving.

How could he possibly have spent that kind of time around her and not know who she really was?

And couldn't the same be said of Cynthia? Twenty-eight years of marriage, and he was not sure he'd known her at all.

And Faith? He'd been wooing her for days. Protecting her. Contemplating a life with her, because he wanted to capture the feeling he had around her.

Of being engaged.

Connected.

Of being alive.

He'd felt he'd been as open and transparent with Faith as he had ever been with anyone. And she thought he was judging her? Not finding her good enough?

It was an insulting misread of him.

But it was certainly more evidence that when it came to the women in his life, he didn't know them at all.

It was good that she was gone, he told himself, because he'd been about to get himself into big trouble with her.

As head over heels—as blindly—in love as he had been when he was eighteen.

He got up from the couch and let himself out of Wolf's Song before his daughter came back.

Faith was exhausted as she walked out of the frosted doors that separated the airline passengers from those picking them up at Toronto Pearson International Airport. She paused for a moment, watching the reunions, people so excited to see one another. Passionate kisses, hugs, greetings.

She realized she was holding up traffic, people streaming around her.

She had to focus on something other than the feeling of her heart breaking. Again. She told herself she had done the right thing.

It wasn't just that she and Brad came from two different stratospheres, that he came from a world that she could barely imagine, and she came from the world that served them.

It was *this*.

This crushing feeling of loss. It was bound to happen sooner or later. Even when someone got a puppy, the sad ending was already looming, waiting…

"Mom!"

Startled, she saw Maggie coming toward her. Her beautiful daughter, her face wreathed in happiness to see her. And just like that, she was part of all of the happy reunions happening around them.

Maggie's arms closed around her. "It's so good to see you."

As if she'd been gone a year, instead of five short days.

"I had no idea you were coming," Faith said. She had fully intended to call a cab. "It's your

busy time of day. Suppertime, and baths, and bedtime stories…"

"I just needed to be here," Maggie said quietly.
"I've been so worried about you." She smiled.
"Not being able to reach you that first day, and
finding out you hadn't checked into your hotel,
sent me into worry mode."

Before Felix, Maggie hadn't had a worry mode.
Now, they all did, like survivors of a terrible natural disaster, an earthquake or a tsunami.

They walked to the carousel and Maggie spotted Faith's suitcase right away, and took it, then
ushered them through the busy airport to her waiting car.

See? Faith told herself. She had family. She
didn't need a man to look after her, to give her
this sense of belonging and home. Maggie was
her home. Maggie was quite capable of spoiling
her on occasion.

She watched how Maggie handled the traffic
with such aplomb, chattering about the girls and
how excited they were as the day care and the
school were already gearing up for Christmas
plays.

"Chloe's been chosen to be the donkey in the
manger scene. She's over the moon. Of course, I
have to listen to her practicing her braying every
waking moment." She demonstrated the bray and
Faith laughed.

It was a reminder that laughter waited, even

after the heartbreak, like sunshine waited behind the rain.

Not that her heart was broken!

She barely knew the man.

Liar, her inner voice reprimanded her.

"I was hoping you could help with the costume," Maggie said. "I don't even know where to begin."

Faith felt a warmth growing in her. Because she knew where to begin. She could already imagine the costume taking shape, the comfort of feeding the nubby gray fabric through her sewing machine.

This was her life. Being with her children and her grandchildren, making cookies and sewing costumes, and being in the front row for the Christmas concerts.

Her life was not erotic experiences at secret hot springs, private zip lines, exquisite meals on mountaintops.

In his heart, Brad knew that. That she could not fit into his world. That was why he had gone to such lengths not to introduce her to his daughter.

They pulled up in front of Faith's house, and Maggie parked in a spot Faith wouldn't have even dared to try. Again, she marveled at her daughter's competence, at the lovely feeling, that despite it all, she and Felix had done so much right.

Maggie brought the suitcase to the front door, and Faith found her key. How would she have gotten in without her purse? She wouldn't have thought about it until just this minute, she'd be standing out here in the cold calling a locksmith.

It had been a miracle, really, that her purse had been turned in.

But where had the miracle been when she had most needed it? No, best not to believe in such things.

Or one could think their first love rescuing them from certain death was also a miracle.

She missed Brad. Crazy to miss him so acutely after just a few days of being with him. On the other hand, when she had seen him after all these years, she had recognized a part of her, a secret part of her, had missed him that whole time.

Maggie was looking at her oddly. "Mom, are you okay?"

Secrets felt as if they took too much energy.

"Have you got time to come in for a minute?" Faith asked her. "I have something I need to tell you."

"Of course, I have time for you, Mom!"

Such a simple statement, and yet it brought tears to her eyes.

"What's going on?" Maggie asked a little later as they sipped hot tea—not fine wine. "I knew I should have gone with you. You shouldn't have tried to look after Grandpa's ashes by yourself. And then losing your purse…"

They sat on the slightly worn love seats in the

living room, facing each other. Faith felt her spirit flitting around her house. She could see the marks on the doorjamb of the upstairs bathroom where they had measured the kids every year. Over there was the spot where Maggie had drawn on the wall with a permanent marker when she was five, and no matter how often they painted over it, it eventually bled through again.

There was the place, on the carpet, where Felix had spilled his coffee, and the dent in the wall where he had fallen.

"I think it's time for me to move," she told Maggie, surprised to realize she had made that decision sometime in the last few days. "The house is at an age where it needs things I can't give it. I've leaned on Sean quite enough over the past few years. He has his own house to look after."

"Don't make that your reason, Mom. We don't mind."

Her memories of the children were imprinted on her heart, not on a growth chart on the bathroom doorjamb.

"It's not the reason," she said. "I'm just ready for a different life."

She and Maggie's phones pinged at identical times. That meant it was either Michael or Sean sending them both a message.

"That's great news," Maggie said, smiling down at her phone.

It was Michael.

I'm going to come home for Christmas. I'd like to
see it one last time, in case it ends up being sold.

The timing of the text seemed serendipitous.
Almost as if, even though the seas separated them,
he had sensed the decision, sensed Faith looking
around that space, getting ready to say goodbye...
their energy joined in ways she would never fully
understand, but was grateful for.

She was aware, as she looked at her phone, it
was quite possible she misinterpreted what had
seemed like Michael's indifference. While she
had been thinking her son was insensitive, was
it possible he was the most sensitive of them all?

"Mom? Is that what you wanted to talk about?
The house? I'm not sad. I was actually hoping
you'd arrive at that decision."

Faith took a deep breath. "No, that wasn't what
I wanted to talk about. I want you to know what
happened the day I arrived in Whistler."

She wanted, suddenly, for her daughter to know
all of it—and maybe all of her—good and bad.
Because wasn't that really what home was, not
four walls, but being accepted for who you were?

So she told her about her ill-advised attempt to
rescue that dog.

As she told it, she was aware she felt it had
been an exceedingly stupid thing to do. On the
other hand, if she had not done it, she would not
have met Brad.

And for all the heartache she was going to feel over the next while, would she trade those days of laughter and adventure and discovery for anything?

The hope they had given her that someday life was going to be okay again.

Maggie was staring at her, open-mouthed. "You broke through the ice and ended up in the lake rescuing a dog?"

Faith nodded. "Please don't say how dumb it was. I already know."

"Is that why you didn't tell me?" Maggie asked softly. "Because you thought I'd think you were dumb?"

Faith nodded. "Getting old. Incompetent. You needing to look after me, instead of the other way around. A repeat of what we went through with your dad."

"Oh, Mom," Maggie said softly.

Faith drew in a deep breath. "There's one more part. The dog's name was Felix."

Maggie was silent for a long time. When she finally spoke, her voice was fierce, and Faith was shocked to see she had started crying when she told her the dog's name.

"Mom, I need you to listen to me. I don't know what's made you feel I think of you like that. Maybe I'm tired sometimes, because of all the things that come from juggling two little kids and a career. Maybe it makes me seem impatient and judgmental.

"But you going out on the ice after that dog? That had Dad's name? That's the bravest thing I've ever heard. You are the bravest person I know. When everybody else, including me and Michael, had given up on him, you hung in there. You got up every single day and did what needed to be done. You went on living, when you must have wanted to just lie down and give up a thousand times.

"You have a warrior spirit. Even when the battles were so hard, even though you knew you could not win, there you were, strapping on your armor and taking up your sword.

"You know what you taught me, Mom? Love can take on anything. Love will get you through things so horrible you cannot even imagine them, let alone prepare for them."

Faith took a sip of tea, stunned by how badly she had misinterpreted how her daughter saw her.

"Speaking of love," she said softly. "There's more. The man who rescued me was Brad Daniels."

"Mr. Hottie," Maggie said, and then it fully registered what her mother had said. "Love?" she squeaked.

"He was my first love, in high school."

And then she told her daughter things she had never told her. About growing up with Max, and working as a maid at the Cobalt Lake Resort, and finally about Mrs. Daniels, letting her know she was not good enough.

And then she told her about Brad spoiling her.

And his daughter finding them in the cottage together, and how she had felt he was ashamed of her.

"Oh, Mom," Maggie said softly. "He wasn't spoiling you. He was romancing you."

CHAPTER TWENTY

FAITH COULD ALMOST allow herself to be persuaded. She had to remember, Maggie was a lawyer. She convinced people of things for a living.

"Until his daughter came along," she said firmly. "And then he couldn't put enough distance between us. I realized he knew I couldn't fit in his world. Ever."

"Out of the hundreds of possibilities," Maggie said gently, "that's what you came up with? Could there be another reason for the way he acted?"

There was that lawyer again!

"I doubt there's another reason for Brad not introducing me to his daughter," Faith said stiffly, almost flinching as she remembered being corrected, and asked to call her Cassandra.

But then she thought, if she was capable of misinterpreting her own son, and her own daughter, had she misinterpreted Brad as well?

"I'm going to tell you what I think," Maggie said, in that tone that let Faith know her daughter was going to tell her, whether she wanted to hear it or not.

"You are that warrior. You are the bravest person I know. But that battle with Dad has left you bloodied and exhausted. And you feel you can't ever do it again. Did you worry if you did hook up with Brad, that you might end up going through it all again someday?"

First of all, she wasn't going to be one-hundred-percent honest after all, because she wasn't going to confide in her daughter she had *hooked up* with Brad, if Maggie was using the term in the way young people seemed to use it.

But, second of all, she was a little surprised that, no, she had never thought of Brad, not even once, of needing her care someday.

Maybe that had been part of his appeal. That he was so healthy, and so vital, the least likely person to ever become dependent.

"You worry about Michael and I, don't you? Carrying the genetic makeup for it?"

As much as she had not thought of Brad in those terms, Maggie hit a nerve with that one.

"I do," Faith admitted, sorry she had not done a better job of hiding that particular concern.

"I did at first, too," Maggie said. "But then I realized all the worrying in the world wouldn't change what was going to happen in the future. All it would do was steal the joy away from today."

"How did you get so wise?"

"Look who I have for parents."

Parents.

"After you've spent your formative years trying to figure out how to keep squirrels out of the bird feeders, believe me, you got some smarts going on."

Faith was so grateful that Maggie had pulled that memory from all of them. She could remember the three of them—Maggie, Michael and Felix—in the backyard, building bird feeders with an impossible-to-penetrate squirrel obstacle course around them. She could remember the laughter, and the intensity with which their latest creation would be observed. In the later years, there had even been cameras set up.

"In my heart, I was always kind of rooting for the squirrel," Faith admitted.

"Me, too. I think we all were."

We.

The family they had been.

It was worthy of gratitude that the last years of struggle had not permanently stolen from Maggie all the incredible gifts her father had given her, when he was still able.

And Michael was going to come, too. He'd called it *home.* She hoped it was those kinds of memories drawing him here.

"See, Mom?" Maggie said quietly. "We'll start to remember the good things again. And that will make us less afraid."

"I suppose," Faith said, hoping for her son and daughter and grandchildren, but dubious for herself.

"You're afraid of loving Brad," Maggie continued, her voice the same soft voice Faith had always marveled at hearing when she explained something to her children. "You're afraid you can't have a happy ending. You're afraid you don't have the strength to battle the uncertainties that love can lay at your doorstep ever again. I think, as brave as you are, you were looking for an excuse to run away from what the universe has given you."

Faith went very still. Regardless of the fact she had never once looked at Brad in terms of health concerns, loving someone took unbelievable courage. She looked at her beautiful daughter, and saw that she was not only wise, but also intuitive beyond her years.

This, too, was what tragedy did—there were roses hidden among the thorns.

"I think you're right," Faith said. "I have no bravery left."

Maggie smiled softly at her. "Sometimes you have to let other people be strong, Mom. I bet Brad has enough bravery for both of you, to carry you until you're strong again."

"I think you're reading way too much into how he feels about me."

"I hope I'm not. That man was absolutely dreamy."

"Well," Cassie told Brad as she came into his office, set a coffee on his desk for him and settled in a chair across from him with her own, "that was an opportunity missed."

He stared at her, startled. Did she mean Faith? How did she know?

"Gregor has been spotted on the French Rivera, with a new girlfriend. They're all gone. Every media person who was here who was interested in that story about your rescue on the lake has disappeared."

He laughed at that. He was pretty sure it was the first time he had laughed in—

"I guess it was time-sensitive, anyway. No one cares about it ten days after it happened."

Ten days. Ten days since he had laughed, since Faith had left, each day longer than the one before it and not just in terms of the winter darkness that was descending on them.

"Ah, well, Cassie, you did a great job keeping them off Gregor's trail for all this time. They still thought he was here, and they had the possibility of that side story to keep them occupied while they waited for a glimpse of him."

"I know," she said with an impish grin, and lifted her coffee cup to him.

He saluted her back. "You're doing a great job getting everything ready for Christmas."

"It isn't a season," she said, "it's a feeling."

He looked out the window. Snow now blanketed his views. He could see skaters on the lake. The trees twinkled with bright lights and decorations.

One season shifted to another. Grief had already taught him that. Everything kept moving, regardless of how you felt about it. He didn't have the *feeling.* But he wasn't going to tell his daughter that, when she was working so hard.

"It's picture-perfect," he said, trying for enthusiasm and missing.

"Dad, is something wrong?"

"No," he said, and then, just barely refrained from adding, *Don't give too much energy to perfection, Cassie.*

"Christmas," she said, cocking her head at him. "It's such a hard time of year. I miss her, too."

"I know, sweetheart."

She looked at her watch, gasped and catapulted from her chair. "So much to do. Oh, by the way, did you get me that cookie recipe?"

"Uh…sorry, no."

She gave him a look of faux annoyance. "Another opportunity missed. Possibly the best cookies I've ever tasted."

And then she was gone. Brad waited until the door had closed behind her, and then, ever so slowly, opened his drawer and took out the letter. He suddenly had to find out if his wife was one more woman he had never really known.

Beloved

Brad was aware of a faint tremble in his hands as he opened the flap of the envelope, the glue long since dried.

A single sheet of folded paper, as yellow with age as the envelope slid into his hands. He closed his eyes, and unfolded the paper.

And then he took a deep breath and opened his eyes.

Beloved, my beautiful girl, you are now hours old and so utterly perfect.

Relief swelled in him, as well as a trace of self-loathing for his own doubts about his wife. The letter was to their newborn daughter.

I am terrified of the huge responsibility you represent. Is there any hope at all of keeping all this perfection intact as you grow toward womanhood? I feel your father and I did not have good role models for this adventure called family that we have entered.

My mom and dad, already gone, were so hardworking and down to earth. But hugs? "I love you"? As foreign to them as a trip to a far-off land. I grew up with "make yourself useful," not "I stand in wonder of your perfection"!

And your grandmother Daniels! I often wonder how did someone so harshly judgmental and so impossible to please, ever raise a man like your father? He is the finest man I've ever known.

My hope for you, darling girl, is this:

From your father, I hope you get qualities of decency, generosity, calm…and the world's best eyelashes.

From me, I hope you get qualities of order and adaptability, an ability to see what could be, instead of what is.

But my greatest hopes aren't about what you inherit from each of us, but what you discover within yourself. I hope you find courage, and independence, and creativity, and joy. I hope as parents, we give you the gift of being you in the world.

And most of all, beloved Cassandra, I hope when love knocks on your door, you say yes to it.

And now, you are stirring, and our new life as a family begins. I am putting this note away for you. I will take it out when you are thirty, and we will look at it together, and see how much of what I have wished for you has come true.

With all my love,

Mom (the happiest word I have ever written)

Brad held the letter for a long time, humbled by his wife's words about him, her words to their daughter.

He looked at the photo of her on his desk. In it, Cynthia was smiling, but he could see the faint tension around her mouth, the faint wall up in her eyes.

It seemed every question he'd had about his wife and their marriage had been answered by what Faith had said, and what this letter confirmed.

His mother had always been a difficult woman. She'd moved from Austria when she was a teenager, but never lost her accent. He suspected she had been made fun of. Once, in a rare moment of softness, Deirdre had told him something that had happened to her own mother during the war.

After that, he'd seen his mother—whom the staff called an old battle-ax behind her back, and the kids at school the dragon lady behind his—in a different light.

She was in some way a tormented soul, and so perhaps he had forgiven her things he shouldn't have. He'd told her once that he would not tolerate her being bad-tempered and judgmental with his wife.

He had never seen her behave that way toward Cynthia again, but after Faith's story, he wondered if he hadn't just forced his mother's aggression underground.

Looking back, he could see the daggers hidden in comments that had been seemingly innocent, that he had not given a thought to at the time. It occurred to him his mother might have subtly— and even not so subtly—tormented Cynthia when he was not in earshot.

And then Cynthia had felt a need to earn her way into the family. She probably had never once stood up for herself, thinking if she was good enough and perfect enough she could win her place in the Daniels family.

He thought of her relentless quest for perfection, the way she had put on airs, and pronounced things *marvelous* when they achieved her impossible standard.

Impossible, because no matter how hard she tried, she had probably never been able to get out from under the harsh judgment of his mother. She had set herself an impossible task if she'd been looking for Deirdre's approval.

It was even possible his mom had been even more ruthless when, after succeeding in getting rid of Faith, she had come up against the exact same challenge a few years later.

Had his mother made Cynthia pay the price for that accidental pregnancy again and again and again?

And he'd been blind to it all, engrossed in his work, thinking Cynthia was just as engrossed in her life, happily turning the resort into a world-class destination, collecting those incredible bottles of wine.

After Cynthia's death, he'd begun to question the strength of their marriage, but now he saw the flaw so clearly.

His mother had bullied his wife, and he had not

seen it, beyond that first time. He should have been more vigilant. Instead, he had not protected Cynthia, not assured her she was absolutely enough exactly as she was.

No wonder, since the early days of their marriage, Cynthia had begun taking those bold midnight skiing excursions.

He'd thought they were out of character for her. She was so controlled, so *not* spontaneous.

But in actual fact, maybe that was the place—the only place—where she had felt free of the oppression of perfection, free to be herself, free to let her hair down, free to scream at the moon if she wanted.

Free to go out of bounds.

Free to shake her fist at all the rules and order that had been imposed on her, first by his mother, and then by herself.

He suspected by the time his mother had died, the patterns had been set. Cynthia had been so far behind the wall of her defenses—making her appearance and the resort and her wine collection so perfect—that she didn't even know that she was behind a wall anymore.

"I'm so sorry," he whispered to the picture. He slid the letter into the top drawer of his desk, added a reminder to his phone for way, way in the future.

He would give it to Cassie, as Cynthia had wanted, on her thirtieth birthday.

He'd known all along that Faith was about second chances to get things right. He just hadn't known how many levels it was on.

He picked up his phone and sent a quick text.

Cassie, are you still nearby? Do you want to walk around the lake with me? I'll tell you what happened that day.

He realized what he was really going to do was ask his daughter's blessing.

She answered back right away.

I'd love that.

Even with her busy schedule, she still loved being with Dad. For all the mistakes he was sure he and Cynthia had made, he could be assured in this.

His daughter was evidence of the triumph of love.

He picked up his jacket and headed out the door. For the first time since Faith had left, he felt optimistic, a stirring of hope chiseling away at the heaviness in his chest.

At the same time, he wondered if what he was about to confide in Cassie meant there was going to be a panic room in his future.

CHAPTER TWENTY-ONE

A PART OF Faith had really hoped that Maggie was right, that Brad had enough bravery for both of them.

But as she clicked off the days of November, it seemed if he was going to be the brave one, there was no sign of it. In fact, that time with him had a dreamlike quality to it, as if it had happened to someone else, unfolded on a movie screen or between the pages of a book.

Real life was enjoying the frenzied excitement of Chloe and Tanya after the first snow. Real life was beginning Christmas shopping, and watching decorations go up, bringing light and color to a dreary time of year.

Real life was helping Michael find a reasonably priced flight to come home.

Real life was starting that donkey costume for the Christmas play, and making paper snowflakes with her granddaughters that were now displayed in every window of her house.

Real life was realizing this would be her first

year without Felix, though in truth, she knew she had lost him a long time ago.

Real life was taking action on her decisions about the house.

The house had actually been too big for her and Felix, once the kids were gone. But she had held on to it knowing that those kind of decisions were beyond his capabilities, and also that the familiar brought him some comfort.

Faith thought, with longing, of the woman she had been for a few short days in Whistler: carefree, bold, sure of herself.

She knew letting go of the house that had brought her such a sense of safety was part of embracing that woman.

That sense of safety had been an illusion. Just like in her dreams, the dangers had lurked, benign, in plain sight.

Yes, on that terrible last day with Brad, she had lost that certainty about herself—given in to old, old insecurities—but she knew now, her confidence was right there, waiting for her to invite it back into the forefront of her life.

A week later, she said goodbye to the real-estate agent, closing the door behind him against the snow that tried to swirl in.

So they would have one last Christmas here. One more time, with the kids and the grandkids gathered around the tree, the house smelling of turkey.

She thought she should feel sad, but she didn't.

As she looked around, she felt oddly free. Selling the house would leave her financially secure for life. That short time with Brad had filled her with longings.

All kinds of longings, she acknowledged with a blush, and yet the one that remained was to embrace adventure.

To travel. To explore. To discover.

The doorbell rang. She thought the real-estate agent must have forgotten something, and went back and opened it. But no, Brad Daniels stood on her doorstep.

He was stunning, just the way she would expect a man to look who had just stepped off his private jet.

But underneath that sophistication, she saw he looked exhausted. Gray stubble—that she had such a desperate need to touch, she had to stuff her hand behind her back—dotted his face. He looked faintly haggard. Thinner.

And then she remembered Maggie saying he would be brave enough for both of them.

His number, from that call Faith had made from the hospital would have been on Maggie's phone.

"Did Maggie call you?" she asked, mortified.

What would her daughter have said? *I think my mom's in love with you.*

And Brad, with his need to rescue…

He looked surprised. "Did Maggie call me? No,

I called her. Her number was on my phone from when you called her from the hospital."

"She knew you were coming?"

"I wouldn't go that far. But she surrendered your address without much of a fight." He smiled that wonderful, delicious, crooked-grin smile at her.

She stepped back and let him in, aware of how humble her house was compared to the opulence of nearly every space at the Cobalt Lake Resort.

But he did not appear in any way aware of the humbleness of her house, just as he had not been aware of the differences in their worlds because of his watch, his car, her luggage, his ability to rent an entire park, or open up a ski hill for a private dining experience.

He had never been aware of those things, so Faith could suddenly see Maggie had been right.

It had been her who had seen the differences in their worlds, it had been her who had jumped to the conclusion that he had not introduced her to his daughter because she was not good enough.

With that realization, Faith felt the door of her heart squeak open one alarming inch.

Just enough that she said, "Come in, Brad. Sit down. Should I make us tea?"

So different than the expensive wines he had offered her. And yet, he tilted his head, and smiled. "Tea sounds wonderful."

And so, a while later, they sat across from each

other, sipping tea from her bone-china thrift-store finds.

Then he set down his teacup, and drew in a deep breath.

"I want to clear the air with you."

"It's not necessary."

"I think it is. I had two reasons to keep you hidden from my daughter, neither of which had anything to do with your perception of not being good enough. First of all, she seemed to think the publicity from my rescuing you would be good for the resort. I knew you did not want Maggie to find out what had happened, so it seemed wise to keep you and my daughter in separate worlds for the time being."

He had been protecting her, Faith thought.

"Secondly, Cassie is very type A. Whatever she does, she does with incredible focus, smarts and zeal. And the very morning of the day I pulled you out of Cobalt Lake, she had indicated that if I was ready to move on, she would be there to *help* me. You cannot even imagine my terror at the prospect."

Faith found herself giggling.

"When I told her I wasn't interested in the awkwardness of dating, she suggested a panic room. A panic room!"

Now, she was laughing.

Oh, how he had a way of doing this to her.

"I was really, really angry when you told me

you thought I hadn't introduced you because I felt you weren't good enough. And when you told me about my mother, my sense of shock and betrayal were off the charts. I had been struggling with a feeling of not really knowing Cynthia, and when you said that, I felt like I didn't know you, either. That I was the worst man ever at reading the truth about women.

"What was the truth about you? Twice, you had let me fall in love with you."

Faith felt her heart stop.

"And twice you had abandoned me. But as a week went by, I realized the truth. There's usually something else underlying anger. And for me, it was fear. Not the let's-jump-off-the-edge-of-the-world kind of fear of zip-lining. A deeper fear. A soul fear of the uncertainties of life. Of how you can think everything is going just fine, and then have your whole world collapse from under you.

"And then I had the thought, if I'm feeling this way, how much worse is it for you? I lost my partner to an accident. But you lost yours in the most cruel way I can imagine. What I realized, Faith, was that it's not about being perceived as not good enough for you. It's the terror of saying yes, once again, to the very thing that tore your world away from you."

Somehow, she was getting up and crossing to him. She found herself, not beside him, but on his lap, her arms around his neck, her tears wetting the crisp white linen of his shirt.

To be *seen* so completely.

"I'm scared, too, Faith. Both of us have learned things do not always go according to our little human plans. But we should have also both learned that life is short. Each breath is precious. We are offered gifts beyond what we can possibly believe we deserve. I want to see where this is taking us.

"I want to explore the physical world with you, but also the world of the heart. I feel we can show each other, and our children, the resilience of the human spirit. We can give them the gift of hope. Yes, bad things happen. Unimaginable things.

"But we pick ourselves up and go on. Not necessarily stronger, but deeper somehow. More compassionate. More in touch. More connected. Not less, not pulling back from the world, but going forward into it, saying a loud, impossible-to-miss *yes*.

"To all of it. The good and the bad."

There, in the circle of Brad's arms, Faith came home. To herself, to her heart, to a world that required the bravery, her daughter had seen, and she had doubted.

Until this very moment.

When he whispered, "Let's embrace our second chance. Let's jump into the abyss, hand in hand. I want you to marry me," she said the only word that was left in her.

"Yes."

EPILOGUE

CASSANDRA STOPPED IN the lobby and took a look around. So much to do, and so little time to do it in. Normally, she probably would have taken out her phone and made a few quick notes.

But the truth was, she was a little disoriented. *She had just met her father's girlfriend.*

Soon to be more than his girlfriend, if the looks Brad and Faith had been exchanging had been any indication.

Dad had sent his company jet to get Faith specifically for them to meet. The meeting had been so touchingly important to him.

Cassandra had thought it might be awkward to meet Faith. The truth? She was just a tiny bit miffed that her dad had managed his own romance without a single bit of input from her.

From the anecdotes around the table tonight, it sounded as if her dad had not only done it without her, but had also absolutely dazzled his new love.

Well, not really his new love. His old love. His high-school sweetheart.

It had been apparent to Cassandra almost as soon as her dad had taken her for that walk around the lake and told her about Faith, that some sort of destiny was at play here. It was powerful that fate had brought them together on the lake, coupled with the odd fact that the dog she had rescued had born the same name as Faith's late husband.

But now, seeing them together, it was so much more than that. Her father and Faith *fit* in some remarkable way.

Even if Faith had not passed her the cookie recipe, she would have recognized her as the woman baking cookies in Wolf's Song. She didn't even want to think of what they had been doing together in there, besides baking cookies!

Still, she could not have conjured someone better for her dad.

Faith radiated a kind of wholesome goodness. She was the type who made cookies, and she had mentioned she was making a donkey costume for one of her granddaughter's Christmas plays. How adorable was that?

There was a sense of family and sturdy values around Faith, and Cassandra found herself loving the fact that Faith made it so apparent she was going to be welcomed into that thing, as an only child, she had always missed. A brother, a sister, nieces!

A sense of home.

But along with that wholesomeness, that sense

of family, there was a kind of quiet strength about Faith. It was the strength of someone who had known suffering and loss as surely as Cassandra and her father had, and decided it was worth it to love again, even if it hurt.

This was the part Cassandra didn't really like: the looks that had flashed between Faith and her dad, the way their hands had intertwined, and their shoulders touched, had filled her with the strangest sensation.

Added to that was how alive her dad had looked. Cassandra wouldn't have even guessed something was missing from his life, until she saw how different he was now that it was there.

It. Love, of course, so evident, shimmering in the air between Faith and Brad like fresh snowflakes twinkling silver in moonlight.

And that strange sensation it had made her feel? She didn't even want to admit what it was.

Not with Rayce Ryan, her own high-school crush, about to arrive here as their newest ski instructor.

It wasn't quite the same. She hadn't been his sweetheart. Ha. She hadn't even been on his radar. And yet, being near him, catching a glimpse of him in a hallway, had always made her heart race and her color deepen embarrassingly.

And then that one night, their final dance ever, as high-school students, it felt as if he had awakened to her.

Seen her.

And for one astonishing moment in time, she had felt as alive as her dad had looked tonight.

And then Rayce Ryan had wanted to kiss her.

And she had run away!

And, of course, in the years that followed, like everyone else in Whistler, she had followed his racing career with avid interest.

But had anyone else experienced that frightening sense of longing that she had nursed ever since she had run away from his kiss?

Had anyone else wanted to coax the tenderness from that devil-may-care man who had challenged the rules of the universe—and gravity—until he had lost?

Impatiently, Cassandra shook off the residue of yearning that seemed to be clinging to her in the face of her father and Faith providing evidence of happily-ever-afters.

Of course, other people had entertained those thoughts about Rayce! He was gorgeous, he was a celebrity, he was a world-class athlete. He'd probably had women, prone to romantic fantasy, throwing themselves at him for close to a decade. Certainly, he had been the heartthrob of at least half the girls in high school, and maybe more!

Cassandra might have secretly indulged the childish notion of endless love when she was young and naive. But she was not that anymore.

She had a million things to do.

A million.

So why was she going back to her place, to look again at all those clippings of Rayce Ryan's career?

Just one more time.

She was just doing her due diligence on the new employee, she told herself, nothing more. Before she put them away.

And before Rayce arrived. A man like that— with all that energy, who had no patience with rules or the laws of order, who was endlessly and effortlessly charming—could turn a world upside down in one blink.

If you let him.

And Cassandra Daniels was not going to let him, not any more than she had let him kiss her all those years ago!

* * * * *

Look out for the next story in the
A White Christmas in Whistler duet

Their Midnight Mistletoe Kiss
by Michele Renae.

And if you enjoyed this story,
check out these other great reads
from Cara Colter:

Accidentally Engaged to the Billionaire
Winning Over the Brooding Billionaire
Hawaiian Nights with the Best Man

All available now!

HARLEQUIN
Reader Service

Enjoyed your book?

Try the perfect subscription for Romance readers and get more great books like this delivered right to your door.

See why over 10+ million readers have tried Harlequin Reader Service.

Start with a Free Welcome Collection with free books and a gift—valued over $20.

Choose any series in print or ebook. See website for details and order today:

TryReaderService.com/subscriptions